Junebug and the Reverend

Also by Alice Mead

Junebug
Adem's Cross

Junebug and the Reverend

ALICE MEAD

Farrar Straus Giroux

NEW YORK

The author wishes gratefully to acknowledge
Sensei Frank DeRaffele of East Asian Martial Arts,
Scarsdale, New York,
for his expert reading of the manuscript.

Distributed in Canada by Douglas & McIntyre Ltd.
Printed in the United States of America
Designed by Judith M. Lanfredi
First edition, 1998
Second printing, 1999

Library of Congress Cataloging-in-Publication Data
Mead, Alice.
Junebug and the Reverend / Alice Mead.—1st ed.
p. cm.
Sequel to: Junebug.
Summary: Having moved out of the housing project and into a new home along with his mother and sister, ten-year-old Junebug discovers that bullies are everywhere and that the elderly can make great friends.
ISBN 0-374-33965-1
[1. Single-parent family—Fiction. 2. Old age—Fiction. 3. Bullies—Fiction. 4. Afro-Americans—Fiction.] I. Title.
PZ7.M47887Ju 1998
[Fic]—dc21 97-48893

For Jeff and Mike—as always

Junebug and the Reverend

One

My birthday dream finally came true. We moved from the Auburn Street projects two weeks ago, from the east side to the west side of New Haven. Now it's Saturday, June 8 to be exact, and Mama's friend Harriet just dropped me off for my third visit to the Fair Haven boatyard.

Here at the boatyard, I'm away from my new school and my new home. The smell of the wind is fresh and salty, and I don't have to worry about bullies or elderly people at all. I, Captain Reeve McClain, Junebug to my family and close friends, am going sailing.

Yeah! This is how it's supposed to be—except that I have to learn boatyard chores, like how to work the smelly old gas pump and how to tie a half-hitch knot.

A half hitch looks like two number eights woven together into a belt-buckle shape.

The boatyard manager is named Ron. He's a big, friendly-looking sort of guy with gray hair and a medium-large belly poking his sweatshirt out in front. He comes walking from a forest of boats resting up on sawhorses. He wipes his hands clean on an old pink towel.

"Reeve, buddy! How ya doing?" he says, shaking my hand.

"Good," I say. "I'm doing great!"

Then he hands me a paint scraper that he pulls from his back pocket. "We're going to do a little work around the yard. After that, we'll go sailing. Fair enough?"

"Sure. I guess so."

Scraping and painting? That could take forever. And I can't wait to get out in the little boat we've been using.

Ron leads me through the forest of boats, and together we start to scrape the barnacles off the hull of a thirty-foot sailboat. Barnacles are little white shelled things shaped like tiny volcanoes with sharp edges around the rim. There are about one thousand of them stuck to the boat. In two seconds, my arms are hurting and I cut my finger. I wipe the blood on my blue jeans. We scrape and scrape.

"Hey, Ron," I say.

"What?"

"Why can't we leave these little barnacles on? Nobody's going to see them underneath the boat."

"This is a lot of work, isn't it?" he says, without looking my way.

"Yeah, I'll say."

"If we didn't scrape off last year's barnacles, then this year's would grow on top of them. Soon the boat would have lumps on its hull, and that would really slow it down in the water. Be ugly as heck, too."

"Ugly only to a fish. Nobody else could see them."

Ron laughs. "I guess you don't like this much."

"No, no. It's okay," I say quickly. I don't want him to think I have a lazy attitude. Mostly I'm curious. Curious about everything, which is how I got my nickname, Junebug. I always pester people with questions, until they just about lose their minds. I'm like a summertime june bug banging on a window screen.

I scrape some more and try to keep quiet. But I can't. A question pops out before I know it. "How long have you worked here?" I ask.

"Here at the boatyard? Oh, about twenty years."

"What? Are you for real? Twenty years?"

"Yeah."

"You came here to work every day for twenty years?" I can't believe it.

"That's right," he says.

"Wow."

My arms are killing me. I let them fall by my sides for a minute to rest. I want to be like Ron.

"So, do you think I could come to work here every day when school gets out?" I ask.

He doesn't answer right off. It's a gusty day, with lots of gray, tattered clouds hurrying by overhead. He keeps scraping and scraping, and I try to keep up.

"I don't know about every day," he says finally. "Maybe."

A few weeks ago, I never thought I'd be here in a real live boatyard. For a whole year, my tenth-birthday wish had been to go sailing. I saved up fifty bottles and put little messages inside each one, asking if I could go for a ride in a sailboat. Then, like a pirate or a shipwrecked guy, I threw the bottles out to sea, and at the last minute my little sister, Tasha, gave my most magic bottle to a ferryboat captain. The captain knew Ron, and now suddenly—here I am! My third Saturday in a row, getting ready to go sailing.

Lately I've been wanting to come down to the boatyard a lot, not just once a week but every day. Especially since there's nothing to do at our new apartment except talk to the old people, Miss Williams and Reverend Ashford. Mama thinks old people are great, but I think they're usually grumpy, and they tell long, boring stories over and over again and talk about recipes for making their mama's gravy, which is a very out-of-date food. Actually, none of this has happened, but I'm expecting it will.

So I hope that when Ron says maybe, he means yes!

Just when I think for sure that my arms are going to amputate themselves, Ron claps me on the shoulder and says we've scraped enough for now. I can't argue with that.

He grabs the crinkly nylon sail bag that we get from a toolshed. The bag is old and spattered with streaks of oil and saltwater stains. We walk toward the end of the dock. I follow his long steps, teetering and tottering, trying to keep my balance, but it's hard. This is by far the windiest day yet.

Before, the wind came in little puffs and the sails hung loosely from the mast. Sailing was a piece of cake, and I wasn't scared a bit. But today! Today the wind is tugging at my shirt, and the water's tossing itself up into little peaks of foam.

Suddenly Ron turns his head. "Can you swim? I know I asked before."

"Yeah. Not real far, though."

"Huh." He keeps walking.

Uh-oh. Why did he ask that? Does he think we might tip over? I bet that's it.

The dock rocks sharply under our feet. Ron turns around again. "There's one rule. Never run. Okay?"

"Yeah."

"Never."

"Yeah."

I'm getting scared. Last week I wasn't. The weather

was so calm. But today the dock is jumping all over the place, rocking and creaking under our feet. I never walked on anything like this before. It sure is no sidewalk. The gusty winds snap at the masts, and metal lines clang nonstop like pot lids banging. Sounds like a grouchy person cleaning up the kitchen.

Way at the end of the dock is our little sailboat, tied up, waiting. It's small. Real small. The first time I saw it, I was a little upset. In my dreams, I always step onto a big, sleek sailing yacht, the kind featured in my sailing magazines, anchored in a quiet coral cove—not a little, banged-up sailboat in cold gray water.

Ron tosses the sail bag aboard and climbs in. Then he reaches out a hand to me. But I'm still having trouble standing on the dock. And I feel kind of frozen to it. I don't want to move my feet.

"Come on," he says, and I reach out. "You'll be okay. This wind is nothing."

We join hands, and all of a sudden I'm standing in the little boat, scared to death. It's maybe ten or twelve feet long. I don't know which, but either way, it's not long enough for weather like this. Gray waves are popping up all around us, slapping the dock and the sides of the boat. I shiver. The water's cold. I can feel how cold it is in the spray. What if we tip over? Oh, man. What am I doing here?

Trying not to look too scared, I buckle on my bulky

life jacket the way Ron showed me the first day. When I turn my body, I feel like a stuffed penguin. No neck, no waist. No wonder penguins don't bend over.

"This boat's not very big," I tell Ron.

He smiles. "Yep, you're right. But you have to start small, don't you?"

"I don't know. You got a bigger one we could borrow?"

He pulls the sail out of the bag and clips it on the mast rope, grinning at me. I sit down on the seat and don't move an inch, hoping to keep the boat steady. Ron is busy with the sail.

"Here," he says. "Pull this rope."

I pull. A second later, the sail rises up the mast, a huge gray-white triangle, flapping, snapping, and tugging in the wind like a live animal full of captured energy. Ron leans way forward and unties the bow rope, then hands me the tiller. Uh-oh, I'm thinking. Does he really believe I can do this? Is he crazy?

"Now, remember, you want to keep the wind coming at the boat from your side, so point the tiller this way," he says, guiding my hand.

I push the tiller away from me a little bit.

Now that we're free of the dock, I can feel the familiar thrill of the water shivering up through the wood and into my hand. When the wind hits the sail full-on, the boat gets a secret life. Half fish, half bird, it's waiting for me to guide it. I ease the rope out a little and hold fast to the tiller. I brace my feet against the opposite seat. My heart is pounding.

We're moving!

When I look back, I see the dock growing smaller and smaller. We're leaving behind everything I know. The boat tilts upward, and we go flying across the water. I'm sailing again! This is my dream come true. All the worries from my new life—about that big kid, Greg, who sits behind me in school, and living with elderly people—these thoughts blow right out of my mind. I'm free!

Ron leans back and stretches out his legs as best he can. He smiles at me, calm as anything.

"There you go," he says. "You're doing real good."

I manage to grin back at him. Captain McClain is at the helm, sailing bravely on course in a full gale. Seagulls circle above the mast. Waves slap the bow and spray the crew with saltwater. Storm's coming up, but don't worry. Nothing scares Captain McClain.

"Hey, Ron," I say, "think I can come tomorrow? Think I can come down here Sunday?"

He looks at me for a moment, then smiles. "Sure," he says. "If you've got a ride."

That's how I know Ron and I are going to be buddies.

Two

At home, I can't stop talking about it. I'm really getting the hang of this sailing stuff. I want to tell Mama everything that happened, every little detail. I told her most of it once, but I want to go over it all again. The thing is, she's been so busy the past two weeks, moving and getting settled in her new job as resident supervisor for a group of elderly patients. Seems she's never really paying attention to me and Tasha anymore.

Well, I've got to be fair. She's paying attention, but in a grownup's way, where only half of her mind is on you, while the other half is on something else—right now, baked lasagna.

So while she's cooking dinner, I follow her around the hot little kitchen, pestering her with the details. She's hunting in the back of the fridge for ricotta cheese, and I'm saying, "I'm getting really good at this sailing business. But you know what one problem is?"

She's bending down, peering into the refrigerator, moving the carrots and margarine and stuff around. "What?"

"I thought maybe I could go down there every day when school gets out. So I asked Ron if I could go tomorrow. He said sure! So can I?"

She finds the ricotta cheese and closes the refrigerator door.

"Can you what?"

She moves to the stove. The big, flat lasagna noodles are already boiling. This could be trouble. Somebody's gotta stir them so they don't stick together in lumps. She hands me a big spoon. I guess that somebody is me. I put on a bulky oven mitt to protect my hand.

"Can I go to the boatyard tomorrow?"

Stay the course, Captain! Don't give up the ship!

"I don't know, Junebug. Don't ask me right now, okay? Ask me after we eat."

I am pretty hungry. Eating sounds like a good idea. But I would rather find out about the boatyard.

"Can we skip putting the lasagna in the oven? Can we eat it unbaked?" I ask.

Who wants to sit around waiting for it to do all that extra cooking? Not me.

"Junebug!" Mama hollers in exasperation. "You're

driving me crazy! Here. Take this box of crackers and go watch TV for half an hour. Please. Go!"

I go into the living area. Tasha, my nearly-six-year-old sister, is having a birthday party on the sofa with her doll babies. That leaves me the rocking chair.

I sit in the chair and have a couple of crackers. They taste good—kind of salty and wheaty. Be nice to have a piece of sharp cheese to go with them.

"So, Mama!" I yell. "Guess how long Ron has worked in the boatyard?"

After dinner, Mama's trying to clean up and I'm helping. Baked lasagna is one of my all-time favorites, but the cheese sure does stick to the pan. Scrubbing the pan reminds me of scraping barnacles.

"Feel my muscles one more time," I say, following Mama from the stove to the sink and back to the stove again. "I'm a guy. I'm all man. I'm Captain McClain."

I push my T-shirt out of the way so she can get a good grip on the brand-new, invisible muscles of my upper arm. She gives my arm another squeeze.

"There. Did you feel that? That's from scraping barnacles. You got to get them off because they can slow a boat down. And did I mention knots? Every time I go, Ron's going to teach me to tie a new knot. Today I started to learn splicing. That's when you join two ropes together."

She stops halfway to the sink, looks at me, and laughs.

"What?" I ask. "It's good to know knots. You start with the half hitch, though. You have to learn that first. Maybe I can teach myself this splicing stuff. That would really surprise Ron."

"Yeah? Well, surprise me first and put the salad away." She hands me the bowl.

"Hey, Mama, you got any wishes? You want me to put one of your wishes in a bottle like I did for my birthday? Look how great this is all turning out!"

Mama puts her hand to her cheek and looks at me as if I caused her a big toothache in her molars. What's she thinking, all of a sudden?

"Junior, Ron's doing us a favor by having you over in the first place. I really don't think he meant for you to—"

I hear someone pounding on the door. "I'll get it." I dance over to open it. "It's probably Miss Williams."

The building where we live now is a home for the elderly. We're supposed to get six old people, all with their own little apartment, but not everyone has moved in yet.

Miss Rosalie Williams is the resident who has the apartment directly across from us. I think she's seventy years old, but you'd never know it. She jogs and stuff. She even lifts tiny hand weights to keep her bones strong. She's cool. Tasha really likes her. I do, too.

But it isn't Miss Williams at the door. It's our other resident, Reverend Ashford, with his grownup son, Walter.

Walter looks older than Mama, maybe thirty. Mama had told us the Reverend was seventy-five. He doesn't dress like a reverend. Instead of a black shirt, he wears plaid shirts and baggy tan pants held up by suspenders because his chest is round, with no waist. You can hear him breathing little, shallow breaths. Once I peeked in his room when the door was open a bit. He has an oxygen tank with plastic tubes that you can clip to your nose.

"Hi, everyone!" says Walter in a loud, cheerful voice. "Sorry to bother you. Is this a good time?"

"Oh, of course. No problem. Come in, come in," Mama says.

I don't think it's such a good time. I was in the middle of a discussion about my future.

Walter's dressed in work jeans and a tucked-in T-shirt that says *Ashford Construction* on the front. There are patches of yellow sawdust still stuck to his clothes from his carpentry job. He drives a blue pickup truck loaded down with ladders and tools.

"We don't want to interrupt, but the doctor adjusted the dose of my dad's blood-pressure medicine this morning."

Walter and my mother head for the charts. Reverend Ashford glares at them for a moment, then reaches into his pants pocket. There's something a little sneaky about the way he does it. He looks almost as if he's getting back at Walter. He pulls out a roll of mints. Maybe he's not supposed to eat candy.

"Guess they don't need us," he mutters, turning his back on them. "Here, you two. Want a mint? I prefer chocolate-covered, but they melt in my pocket."

"Sure," I say.

Tasha doesn't answer. That's usual for her with someone she doesn't know.

"I didn't want to move here, you know. Walter and my doctor made me. Had to sell my house. My wife and I raised six children in that house. Lived there for thirty-eight years."

Wow. That's longer than Ron has worked at the boatyard.

His voice gets shaky. I hope he doesn't cry—I won't know what to do. Why did we have to move in with old people, for Pete's sake? How do you play with someone who's seventy-five?

Reverend Ashford opens a new mint pack and peels down the foil wrapping. He gives me one, then stares at Tasha. "When is she going to say something?" he asks.

"I don't know. She doesn't talk much to anybody."

"She doesn't, eh?"

"Except to Rosalie," says Tasha.

"What's that?" exclaims Reverend Ashford.

"Rosalie. Miss Williams," Tasha says loudly.

"Miss Williams, across the hall," I explain. "She and Tasha are friends."

"Do you like Miss Williams?" Tasha asks.

"I hardly even know her," he says.

Suddenly Reverend Ashford hands Tasha the whole pack of mints. "Here."

He glances at Walter and Mama. They're talking and laughing over at the dining-room table.

"What on earth's keeping them?" he asks.

"I don't know," I say. I'm wondering the same thing myself.

Tasha takes a mint, puts it in her cheek, and sucks hard on the candy. When Tasha finally does something, she doesn't mess around.

"Where'd your front teeth go?" Reverend Ashford asks.

"I lost 'em," she says. "The tooth fairy came and I got a dollar."

She sticks the white mint where her teeth used to be and grins at Reverend Ashford as if she's a pumpkin. He laughs and sits down in the rocker. I feel pretty lucky to have Tasha for a sister and not somebody else.

"Is it seven o'clock yet?" she asks. "I gotta go."

Tasha doesn't wait for the Ashfords to leave or anything. She marches straight across the hall and bangs on Miss Williams's door.

Reverend Ashford gets to his feet. "I'm going back to my apartment," he says. "See you all tomorrow."

He leaves and there I am, watching Mama and Walter. I realize I have a problem. Mama loves her new job. And now it seems she might like more than her job, and that Tasha and I might be coming in third.

I throw myself into the rocking chair. Tasha and Miss Williams are getting along great. But who am I going to hang around with? Actually, when Mama took me to sign up for my new class at school, the teacher, Mr. Olson, said there was a boy my age, Brandon, who lived nearby. I've seen him at school all right. He's scrawny and shy and doesn't play with anybody at all. He's supposed to be my new friend?

Walter glances my way and smiles. "I took a little time off work this afternoon, and I took my dad to a double-A baseball game. The New Haven Ravens. That's a funny name, isn't it?" he says to me.

"Yeah. I guess so." I can't smile back.

I know he's trying to be nice. I wish I felt a little bit friendly, but I don't. And then, worse yet, I remember Walter's pickup truck and think that's how I can get to the boatyard. I know it's not very nice of me to ask a favor, but I have no choice.

Mama gets up and puts Reverend Ashford's file away. Still, Walter doesn't leave. Instead, he and Mama sit at the table, smiling at each other. I head on over and start examining the corner of the table.

I can feel something powerful in the room, something swirling in the air between them. It's not that they're saying much to each other. Truth is, they hardly say anything at all. But I can feel their hearts jammed full of happiness at that moment, and it has nothing to do with me or Tasha.

Finally, Walter gets up to go home.

This is my one and only chance. I clear my throat. "Um, Walter, do you think you could give me a ride tomorrow? I mean, I know it's Sunday, but I wondered if you could drive me to the boatyard. It's called Fair Haven boatyard. It's not very far from here."

"Reeve!" Mama exclaims. "I'm sorry, Walter."

But Walter just laughs. "No, it's okay. Look at all you're doing for my dad. He's done nothing but sit in a chair for the past six months. Already he's up and around. I'd be glad to help out. What time do you want me to pick you up?"

"One o'clock would be real good," I say.

"Sure, I can do that. See you all." And he leaves.

"I don't know about you, Junior," Mama says. "Are you sure it's all right with Ron for you to go down there again?"

"Yep," I say, widening my eyes and giving a great big nod. "Hey, I gotta call Robert and tell him about sailing."

Robert is my best friend from Auburn Street,

where we used to live. What with one thing and another, I've only called him twice since we moved.

I go into Mama's room to use the phone. But Robert's line is busy. That probably means his mother is home. She talks on the phone for hours. Then I leave and go to my room. I forget all about asking Mama if I can go to the boatyard every day during the summer. Tomorrow's good enough for now. I flop down on my bed.

I stare up at the ceiling and pretend that, somehow or other, it turns out that Ron's my dad.

Now, that would be cool. Me and my brand-new dad, Ron, out sailing.

Three

Sunday gets off to a real bad start. I wake up and see that it's sunny, and I smell bacon frying. That's the good part. That's the only good part.

It's still early when Mama opens the door. "Junior," she says, "I have a great idea."

"Oh, yeah? About the boatyard?"

"No. About Reverend Ashford. This summer, early every morning, I want you to take him for a short walk."

"Every day?" I squeak.

"Yes."

I can't believe it! I keep my eyes closed.

"Junior, are you resting? You need to get up," she says. "I want you and Reverend Ashford to go out before it gets too hot."

She's not kidding! This is for real!

Oh, man. What if the guys back at the project saw me doing this? Or even the boys at my new school? I have two jobs now. One of them working at the boatyard and one of them exercising a reverend.

"Do you want some blueberry pancakes with your bacon?" Mama asks.

I can't say no to blueberries. Or any berry. She knows that. This pancake thing is blueberry bribery. I get up.

After I eat, Mama tells me to wait outside while she gets Reverend Ashford. I stand on the front walk, feeling groggy. Who wants to wake up? Not me. But I'm a cheerful person. And it's hard work for me to stay in a bad mood for long.

This will be a good day, I decide. I'm going down to the boatyard in the afternoon. And maybe Mama thinks exercising the Reverend is a way to pay Walter back for driving me. I can accept that.

I wait and wait. Finally, after about twenty minutes, here he comes. Mama, too.

"Today," says Mama, "we're only going to take a little walk down Robin Lane and around the circle, just to see how it goes."

Robin Lane is about three hundred feet long. After we walk down the street, back up, and then around the circle once, though, she makes us do it again. We're doing laps, all three of us! Oh, man.

"This is too much. Much too far," Reverend Ashford grumbles.

"Not at all. You're doing fine," she tells him. "Why do you think this is too hard for you? The doctor never told you that. I bet it's because you want to sit some more in your chair, right? Well, we need to get you up and moving. You can't watch game shows for the rest of your life."

Maybe not, but it sure seems that's exactly what he was thinking of.

"What are you looking at?" he says to me.

"Me? Uh, nothing, I guess."

He snorts.

From down the street, I see a puny little white kid coming along Bellmore Avenue on a bike.

"Is that the boy from your class?" Mama asks.

"Yeah," I say shortly. "That's him. That's Brandon."

"Well, it'll be nice to have a new friend so close by."

I like to choose my own friends. But it seems that since we moved here Mama and I don't agree on that.

"All right, Reverend," says Mama. "Three times around and you can go back to your room, just like I promised."

We walk up the path. She opens the front door for him and he goes stumping down the hall to his room. Apartment 6-A. Our whole building is the A building. B and C aren't done yet.

When he's out of sight, Mama smiles at me and says, "There you go. Tomorrow, he's all yours."

My legs feel saggy and I lean against the doorpost. Seems there's no way I can get out of this. No way at all.

After lunch, Walter comes right on time to get me. I climb into the truck.

"Wait a second. I'm going to try to bring my dad along for the ride."

What? Oh, no.

Walter disappears into the building. A few minutes later, he comes out with Reverend Ashford.

I squeeze over and sit in the middle. Walter helps his dad climb in.

"Not you again!" says Reverend Ashford when he sees me. "You're ruining my life, young man. Exercise. Boatyards. What else have you got up your sleeve? I'm not supposed to be out in this heat. Doctor's orders."

"Dad," says Walter patiently, "it's only eighty today. And you're out of the sun. You'll be fine. You have to have some confidence."

But I guess Reverend Ashford doesn't want to have confidence. He doesn't say one word all the way to the boatyard. At a red light, Walter smiles at me and shakes his head.

Down at the boatyard, the sun is sparkling on the water and the little waves are a bright, bright blue—completely different from yesterday. As Walter drops me off, I get so excited that I leap from the truck and go tearing down the driveway. Halfway to Ron's office, I realize I forgot to say thank you for the ride.

I cross the rickety wooden boardwalk that leads to the boatyard office door and go inside. Ron is at his desk, on the phone, and he looks surprised to see me at first. But he won't mind when he sees what a big help I'm going to be.

"Hi!" I call out loudly. I might be interrupting.

"Oh, yeah. Hey, Reeve. Be right with you, buddy."

I wander to the window, then go outside to wait. The boatyard was nearly deserted yesterday in the cold gray weather. But today is warm and sunny, and it's mobbed. There are cars parked everywhere. I hear saws screeching and radios blaring, and I can smell sawdust all over the place from people sanding down wood and revarnishing it.

I liked it better yesterday when nobody was here. Once I got used to those strong, gusty winds, I thought the weather was exciting.

I sit down to wait. Maybe I did push Ron too much to let me come again. I bet I junebugged him. He's probably busy with all these folks around. It's just that I had so much fun being with him yesterday. My real dad we don't see anymore. Mama doesn't even call him. He's in prison in upstate New York or Massachusetts, I think. I've kind of forgotten. It's been six years since I've seen him. He left just before Tasha was born. I scuff a dusty hole in the dirt with the toe of my sneaker.

"Hi!" a girl says, going past me with a friendly smile. She has short, swinging brown hair that gleams in the sun. I say hi back. I'm generally pretty friendly.

Some boat-owner people come along the little boardwalk and go into the office. They are all wearing brown loafer shoes with white string laces tied in front.

A minute later, Ron comes to the door with a ring of keys. There must be about twenty of them on there.

"Listen, Reeve, I'm still on the phone. Can you show these people where the storage shed is? It's where we stowed the sail bag yesterday. Here. Here's the key."

I show them the shed, and they pull out some enormous extension cords. Then I relock the padlock and go back to the office. Ron's at the door, waiting.

"Hey, buddy, I don't think I'll be able to spend much time with you today. A boatyard depends entirely on the weather. Weather is king around here. Weather's my boss."

I try to smile. I want to hide my disappointment.

"So, what do you say we split a soda?" he asks. The soda machine is outside the office door. "You like root beer?"

It's not my favorite, but it's okay. While I'm sipping, I notice that on his arm, the inside, pale part, is a blue-green rose. It's a tattoo.

"How come you have that?" I ask.

"Oh, I don't know. I got it a long, long time ago. It reminds me of things."

"What things?"

"I don't know. Mistakes I've made, maybe. I had it done during a bad period of my life."

I look at it more closely.

"Those lines are skinny as a pin."

"Yeah, well, they're made by a pin. A pin that injects ink."

"Ow! Doesn't that hurt?"

"Of course it hurts. Listen, I have to get back to work. You want to call your mother and have someone pick you up?"

"Yeah, I guess so. Can I come by here tomorrow after school?"

"Not tomorrow. Let's try for Saturday, all right?"

I nod, then go inside the office to call Mama. She says Walter will be by for me in half an hour. So I go wandering down on the docks. I see the little sailboat we use, still tied up at the end. It's bouncing on the blue water, looking happy. Wish I was feeling happy.

Well, I bet next Saturday will be fun. Ron'll be ready for me for sure, and maybe we'll sail out really far. He'll have so much time for me that maybe we'll sail all the way to West Africa or Timbuktu.

Four

"Please, not today. Not today, Mama. It's the last week of school. Can't he walk himself?" I beg.

Now it's Monday. Mama's still getting on my nerves. Walking Reverend Ashford yesterday was no fun at all, even with Mama along. He sulks worse than I do! I do not want to do it again.

"Twenty minutes and you can come right back," she says.

It's ten minutes after seven. Miss Williams has already come back from her morning exercise, wearing her snazzy purple-and-gold-sparkle jogging suit. Now she's in her apartment, stretching. She may jog real slow, maybe one mile per hour, but she's spunky. She even jogs in the rain.

Mama said that Reverend Ashford has emphysema,

which means his lungs are damaged. He gets tired and he coughs, and air pollution is bad for him. I have to take him for a walk to keep his lungs strong. And I'm supposed to talk to him so he'll become more sociable.

Oh, man. Here he comes. We meet out on the front sidewalk, both of us frowning.

"Have a nice time," Mama says. "Why don't you take Brandon along? He's just down the street." Then she shuts the door. Bam!

Oh, man.

"Your mother is a strong woman," Reverend Ashford says, looking at the closed door.

I think he might be right. Stubbornness runs in the family, I do know that. Now that he mentions it, it seems that Mama is getting stronger and stronger every day since we moved to this place. Back at our old apartment in the Auburn Street projects, she acted tired and a little sad most of the time. But here she's perky. And when she's perky, watch out!

Our group home is on a brand-new dead-end street. In the middle of the turnaround area is a tiny park, a circle of grass with a sidewalk and three cement benches. Right now, the only person who uses the park is Tasha, when she takes her babies for a stroll. She sits them on the seats and feeds them blades of torn-up grass and dandelions for lunch.

Our big problem is that there's nowhere in particular for us to go. This isn't really a neighborhood; it's more of an industrial area with housing for the elderly thrown in. Cranston Road goes up the hill behind the apartments, past the bakery. But Reverend Ashford doesn't like walking uphill because of his breathing, so that's out of the question. And going down Bellmore Avenue isn't a whole lot of fun. Early in the morning, a ton of trucks drive by, and it's pretty ugly. Truck city. But there *is* a corner store on Bellmore near Brandon's garage.

A couple of times since we moved, I've spotted Brandon's dad outside the garage, repairing cars. But I've never seen Brandon helping him.

The Reverend and I decide to walk to the store to buy a newspaper. On our way out of the store, Reverend Ashford slips me some money. Two dollars and fifty cents.

"Get me a pack of cigarettes, will you?" he says. "Camels."

"Huh? Are you allowed to smoke?" What's he doing? Isn't smoking like indoor air pollution?

"What do you mean? Of course I'm allowed. I'm an adult. I can smoke a few cigarettes a day. No one has to 'allow' me. I 'allow' myself."

"Okay. If you say so." I go back inside the store. "Can I have a pack of Camels?"

"We don't sell to minors," the old guy at the counter says. "Now scoot."

"But they're not for me."

I look around for Reverend Ashford. He waves at the store man. A minute later, I walk out with a pack of cigarettes.

Reverend Ashford smiles. He opens the crinkly cellophane wrapper and lights up. He pulls in so hard on the tobacco that the cigarette burns down in no time. He smokes a second one real fast. And then he pulls out a packet of mints from his pocket.

Hey! I've seen those mints before! I bet they make his breath smell better. That makes me wonder again.

"Reverend Ashford, are you sure it's okay for you to smoke?"

"Are you my doctor?" he asks. "Do I have a ten-year-old doctor?"

"No."

"All right, then. And I don't need any ten-year-old doctor. Trust me. What my habits are, that's my business, not yours."

But I won't quit asking. "Does my mama know?"

"Of course she knows. Now you get on with your life and leave me to mine. There's no need for you to mention this ever again, all right?"

"Okay."

I guess if you don't tell on kids, you sure as heck shouldn't tell on grownups.

We start back along Bellmore. Delivery trucks, oil trucks, tow trucks, vans all whiz by us. I peek at Brandon's house. He lives upstairs, where there are two windows, above his dad's car-repair shop. It always looks as if no one's home. The washed-out curtains never move. I wonder why not.

After we get to Robin Lane, we sit on the cement benches, reading the newspaper. I head for the comics; Reverend Ashford heads straight for the sports page. He wants to see how much the players are paid. It's getting hot and steamy, so we fan ourselves with the classifieds. We're not allowed back inside until twenty of eight. This is pure torture. I give a big, fat sigh.

I wonder what kind of summer this will turn out to be. My teacher at school, Mr. Olson, is organizing a city-wide soccer league with some other schools, with parent coaches, but I don't want to do that. What I'd been hoping to do was sleep in good and late, rent some movies, work at the boatyard, invite my buddy Robert over, go to the beach once or twice. Doing this walking thing early every morning is cramping my style.

Reverend Ashford folds up the newspaper and looks around.

"You know what this place needs?" he says as the hot sun fills the sky with a hazy glare.

I don't know exactly, but I can tell it needs something.

"Trees. How can they name this place Robin Lane

when there's not one single place for a bird to sit and rest his wings?"

"I don't know."

"We ought to plant some. Stop this walking nonsense and plant some trees."

"How do you get a tree? Dig one up?"

"They sell 'em. A pin oak would be nice. Or birch."

"A dog would be nice," I say.

"What's that? A dogwood?" Reverend Ashford says. He doesn't always hear right.

"No! A dog. You know. It barks and wags its tail."

People usually have to walk a dog. I'm the only person in the whole entire world who has to walk a reverend.

"Of course I know," he says in a grouchy voice.

I don't say anything after that. He always starts to feel sad when he doesn't hear something right. He has a hearing aid, but he won't use it.

He says, "I used to have a parish with a congregation of five hundred people. Now look at me."

"Yeah? You're doing all right," I say in a loud voice, so he'll be sure to hear. "You're hanging out with me, anyway."

He snorts but he doesn't answer. It's funny; the last time he told me about his congregation, he said it had eight hundred people in it. And one time he told me he had six children. Another time he said he had three. Talking to Reverend Ashford is confusing.

"Think it's twenty of eight yet?" He pulls out an old gold pocket watch on a little chain. The top flips up. The watch face has those roman numerals. Nothing digital about it.

"Five more minutes," he says.

"I have a job down at the boatyard," I say then.

"Oh? Well, that's good. Always good to have a job."

"Yeah. I really like it."

"Play any sports?" he asks. "Any baseball?"

"No."

"My son Walter loves baseball. Always trying to get me to go to a game."

After a while I say, "Mama wants me to play soccer."

"I guess you better go on and do it, then."

Hey! That's not what I wanted to hear!

He stands up, ready to go back inside on the dot, when the time finally comes.

"Today's your library day," I say, looking at the date on the top of the newspaper.

He mutters something about never being left alone now that he lives here. "It's too hot to go anywhere," he says. "There's too much pollution."

"The library's air-conditioned," I remind him.

He checks his watch again. "Twenty of!" he says. "That's it! Come on. Let's go."

As soon as I'm inside, I complain to Mama about taking Reverend Ashford on his walk. She barely listens.

"But he doesn't want to do it, either."

"It builds character to do things you don't want to do," she says. "It's good for both of you. A little exercise is a great way to start the day. Look at Miss Williams."

Now, how are we supposed to keep up with Miss Williams? She's a human fireball.

I snatch up my schoolbag. "Come on, Tasha. We're going to be late for school, the way things are going!"

Mama hands me my lunch. I can tell she's thinking. "Junior, isn't there something going on at the school tonight? Some special event? Is it a fundraiser? I've been awfully busy. I wonder what . . . Where's that soccer sign-up sheet? I think a flier came home with that."

"Oh, yeah. Well, umm, I think the time's about up on the soccer sign-up. Besides, parents are supposed to come to the practices, and you're pretty busy right now," I say quickly. "I don't think you'd have time."

I'm staring at the group of red-and-white bakery trucks pulling out of the parking lot behind our apartment, all set to make their morning deliveries. I don't want her to remember. Tonight's the parent-child spaghetti dinner to raise money for the summer soccer league. After she read the flier, I hid it.

All the boys in the class are showing up for the dinner with their dads. At least they say they are. A lot of the kids' parents are divorced, probably about half of them, but they visit their dads and stuff.

Not me. How can I do that? I can't get my dad out of prison. I can't get him to come up for the weekend. I can't even tell him about sailing with Ron or working down at the boatyard. And I don't want to be the only kid to show up with my mom. I don't want anyone asking where my dad is. Not at this school. Not with these kids, who don't even know me. Besides, no one here at King cares if I show up or not. No one's begging me to be on his team.

"Bye!" I yell and slip off up the street. "Come on, Tasha."

She has to run to catch me.

Five

As usual, skinny old Brandon, who sits next to me, hurries in just *after* Mr. Olson finishes taking attendance. And, as usual, Mr. Olson doesn't say one word about it. I wonder why that is. I like to know what's going on. This is a mystery that I, the ever-curious Junebug, will have to investigate.

"Okay," says Mr. Olson. "Last call. Do I have all the slips for the parent-child spaghetti dinner tonight?"

I glance at Brandon. He's the only other kid in the class who didn't sign up for the dinner or for soccer.

"Those should have been turned in on Friday," Mr. Olson continues. "I think I've got just about everybody's. Any latecomers? Reeve, how about you?"

I shake my head and look down at my math workbook. I try not to think about any dumb old parent-child spaghetti-dinner thing. Anyway, who likes soccer? I've hardly ever played it before, except once or twice in gym. I've got the boatyard to keep me busy. If I need to spend time with a father, I can pretend Ron's my dad. It would be so cool to have a dad who ran a boatyard.

It's not important to come to a school dinner. Only Mr. Olson thinks so. And maybe Mama. But we never did that kind of community stuff at my old school, so why start now?

We just got assigned two pages of long division. Well, not that long—only two numbers—so it's more like medium division. But it's still hard for most of the kids. Not for me, though.

Brandon hasn't started yet. He always looks lost, like a rabbit at the mall pet store. Seems none of the kids really like him. He's not doing the math problems at all—just sitting, staring at the paper as though it's not really there. There is something on that kid's mind for sure. I wonder what. Suddenly he gets up, takes the bathroom pass for the boys' room off the hook, and heads on out the door.

Behind me, two boys, Darryl and Greg, start to snicker. They're whispering, and Darryl passes something to Greg. Then Greg gets up to sharpen his pencil. Well, wouldn't you know, he has to walk right past Brandon's desk to get there. On his way by Brandon's chair, he leaves two thumbtacks on the seat, pin side up.

Greg sharpens his pencil in less than one second. Then he sits back down. I turn around and stare at those guys. Darryl's skinny and weak-looking, but Greg's a big kid. He's huge. He's a tank. Brandon's so puny that it doesn't seem fair for anybody to pick on him. What's the point? I give them a frowny look that says, Grow up!

"What are you staring at?" Greg says to me in a loud whisper.

Mr. Olson glances our way.

In my old school, it wasn't cool to pick on little kids, but this is only my third week here at King, so I just shrug and get back to my work. Brandon returns, and he sits right down on those tacks. He glances once at Greg and Darryl, as if he knows it's them. Then he starts to cry. He puts his head down on his arms.

Mr. Olson goes over and whispers to him, and takes the tacks in the palm of his hand. Then he straightens up and looks at all of us over in our corner of the room. "Who did this, fellas?" he asks.

Now everyone is doing long division.

"Hey!" he says sharply. "Somebody must have seen something."

I look around. Nobody's talking. Math suddenly got real popular. I guess everybody's thinking they need math for their future careers. I sit still, sneaking glances at Brandon to see what he'll do next. He's got to do something about this. He can't just sit there with the sniffles, but that's what he does.

Be brave, kid, I want to holler. Be brave!

He doesn't move a muscle. Now, see? He's got a dad. I've seen him working on cars down in his repair shop. Somebody's gotta teach Brandon how to stand up for himself and not get pushed around. Gotta teach him how to be a man. This is the moment when you have to dig in your heels, no matter what.

"Reeve? How about you?" Mr. Olson asks. "Do you have something to say?"

"No," I say softly.

I want to tell Mr. Olson he's got two great big cowards sitting behind me. Their initials are D. and G. But I don't say anything. I know the other kids are watching me. I wonder if they did this, they hurt Brandon, just to see what I would do. In fact, I'm sure that's why they did it—to find out whose side I'm on. Probably because I get good grades, they want to see if I'm a softie, a kiss-up.

At my old school, my best buddy, Robert, and I always got good grades, even in homework. We did well in school and got good-attendance awards, too. Nobody gave us a hard time for it as long as we didn't brag. Here it seems as if all the boys are trying to do medium-bad. That way, none of them stands out at either end.

Mr. Olson gives up trying to find out what happened and goes back to his desk.

At the end of math, I place my open workbook on the pile with everyone else's. Just as I turn to go back to my seat, Greg bumps into me on purpose and steps on my big toe really hard.

"Hey!" I say, plenty loud. "Watch where you're going!"

Mr. Olson is on us in a second, frowning. He didn't see what happened, but he senses trouble. A lot of teachers are like that. They can tell when something's up.

"Greg, Reeve," he says, looking from one of us to the other. "What exactly is going on today?"

"Nothing was going on till this kid got in my way," Greg says.

Greg is wearing droopy denim overalls over a sagging T-shirt. He has a pierced ear with a hoop ring in it. He must think he's on MTV. I'm in my usual pair of gym shorts and T-shirt. Nothing fancy.

"I didn't get in anybody's way, including yours," I say, calm as stones.

Greg and I are staring at each other. Now I'm as angry as he is.

"The two of you have a choice. You can take your seats and drop this," Mr. Olson says. "Or I can help you settle it after school. This pushing and shoving will not take up our class time. Greg?"

"We don't need no help," Greg mutters and heads toward his seat. He falls into his chair like an overcooked noodle. Mr. Olson goes back to his desk with the big, floppy pile of workbooks.

As I reach my seat, I whisper, "I don't need help with somebody who puts thumbtacks on another kid's chair."

"Yeah?" Greg says. "Well, I don't need help with a kid that tries to tell me what to do. That's what I call disrespect."

Oh, man. I hate that word. The "D" word. We're in trouble now. Stands for "no big *deal*" to me.

I have no interest in backing down or shaking hands or any of that. Kids as sneaky as Greg don't scare me. I wish he were smaller, though.

"What you did to that kid, Brandon, was wrong," I say, turned around in my chair. "That's all I have to say."

"Yeah? Well, it's enough. Meet me at three o'clock . . ."

"Let's line up for recess," Mr. Olson calls out.

"Did you hear me?" Greg whispers.

I nod, trying to look cool as a cucumber. Inside, I'm shaking. Who wouldn't be?

Starting a new school in June is not much fun. Everybody is already busy, especially the teacher. At the end of the year, it seems that all teachers do is snatch up their papers and rush out of the classroom to meetings. That means the teacher next door has to come by and poke his head in because he has to watch two classes at once. Fifty kids! There is *a lot* of yelling. When no one's watching, kids like to hang out the window and feel the summery air on their faces.

Mr. Olson's not as sweet-natured as my old teacher, Miss Jenkins, but Mama says I haven't given him half a chance. She says I haven't given the elderly people in our group residence a chance, either. Well, Miss Williams is pretty nice, but Reverend Ashford is a real grouch. And neither one of them makes up for Robert and my other friends from Auburn Street.

But here's a good thing about Mr. Olson. He comes out to play kickball with our class at least once a day. When he boots the ball, it sails up in the air way over the fence, and the kids yell.

"That ball is in orbit. It's headed for the moon!"

"Maybe Mr. Olson's an astronaut. Hey, Mr. Olson, are you an astronaut?"

"He's no astronaut. He's been working out. Isn't that right, Mr. Olson?"

"No, he doesn't. Teachers are weak. Teachers don't work out."

"Mr. Olson does. My cousin saw him. He lifts down at the Y gym."

Maybe he works out, but I think the wind has caught the ball and taken it sailing up into the clouds. I'm a sailor. I know the magic the wind can do.

Mr. Olson says recess is the most important part of our day. That's when we learn to treat each other with respect. He demands it, and he gets it most of the time because he plays fair. I guess I do like him. I'm starting to, anyway. That's why he does the summer soccer league—to make kids play fair and win using teamwork, not violence.

After recess, all the big kids swirl around him as they come up the stairs, hot and sweaty from kickball. Everyone laughs and talks and feels good. But no one in my new school knows my nickname, Junebug. They don't call me Junior, either. Mr. Olson calls me Reeve. Nobody else calls me anything.

At lunch, sitting all alone, the other kid who always has to eat by himself and pretend he doesn't care is good old Brandon. He usually sits two tables away from me. His problem isn't a race thing. It's more that he's given up on everything. He doesn't care about his schoolwork or recess or what's in his lunch bag or anything. I can see his skinny little neck poking up through the neck hole of the droopy gray sweatshirt he wears to school every day.

Brandon, man, that kid needs a trip to the boatyard. He needs to lift weights or learn karate or something. He needs some kind of self-defense, some protection, or someday somebody's going to snap that kid in two like a toothpick.

I don't think kids should pick on weaklings like Brandon, but if I go eat lunch with him and try to cheer him up, then he'll probably turn into a great big Mr. Tag-a-long and follow me around for the rest of my entire life, and that would mean nobody else in the school would ever be friends with me. So I stay where I am. The Cowardly Lion, that's me.

I'm feeling pretty nervous about later this afternoon, and it's hard to swallow my sandwich. I manage to eat about half of it, which, for me, isn't much. I give a big sigh and toss my crumpled-up bag into the trash barrel, then lay my head on the table, waiting to be dismissed.

I miss my buddy, Robert. Mama kept telling me this school would be so much nicer than my old one. But just because it has carpets and a swimming pool and it's in a safer neighborhood doesn't make it perfect. Greg reminds me of a mean kid at Auburn Street named Trevor. I guess kids can become bullies even when they have fancy new overalls and moms who pick them up in minivans. Bullies like Trevor and Greg pop up everywhere.

Robert's mother was hardly ever home. She said she was a waitress and had to work late at night. But Robert's the sweetest kid I know. He wouldn't hurt a fly. There's no excuse when it comes to hurting people.

And me? I try hard to be good, and my dad's in jail!

For robbery. Armed robbery. But I know right from wrong. At Auburn Street, everybody knew about my dad, but they still cared about me. Not here, though. Nobody cares. But I don't want anyone here to know. Forget spaghetti dinners. Forget soccer. I just want to go to school, go home, do my homework, keep my grades up, and talk to nobody if that's how it's got to be.

Maybe I should have kept quiet this morning and let that nasty old Greg do whatever he wanted. Being a Junebug, though, it seems I always have to butt my head in. No matter what, sooner or later I speak up.

I have no idea what will happen after school with Greg and his dumb friends. Thinking about it gives me a heavy, dreadful feeling. Maybe I ate a big rock for lunch. A rock sandwich.

Six

The terrible afternoon drags on. The clock hands don't move. Behind me, Greg keeps leaning over and whispering to Darryl.

Finally, Mr. Olson says, "Greg, that's it. I want you to sit up front for the rest of today."

"What?" squeaks Greg. "What did I do? Come on, Mr. O., I didn't do anything."

Greg doesn't move. "Please?" he whines. "I promise not to bother anybody."

But Greg made a big mistake. He whined! Mr. O. hates whining more than anything. He points to the NO WHINING sign above the blackboard and says, "Let's go. Move it."

Greg moves one arm and half moves the other. His butt stays still.

Mr. Olson says in a steely voice, "Greg, your choice is to move on your own or with my help. Which will it be?"

Shoulders down, looking miserable, grumbly old Greg slouches up front and sits down.

Mr. Olson says, "Now I have a reminder for everybody. Some of you haven't turned in your soccer sign-up sheets, and school vacation starts Wednesday at noon. I have a sign-up list here for the city-wide soccer leagues. For both boys and girls. The boys play here at school four mornings a week. The girls will play at Farrington Elementary. There are play-offs, prizes. A great way to stay in shape. How many had older brothers and sisters in this last year?"

A scattering of hands go up.

"They loved it, didn't they? I urge each and every one of you to talk this over with your folks. I want you kids involved in something, doing something. Turn off the boob tube and get out and run around!"

"Soccer's for white kids," mumbles Greg just loud enough for Mr. Olson to hear.

"It is not, Greg," says Darryl. "My dad's going to be assistant coach. He was on a championship team in Jamaica."

"Soccer is a universal sport, played widely in every country of the entire world," Mr. Olson says calmly. "Greg, your mother has already signed you up. The rest of you, make sure your sheets are back and signed by tomorrow."

I'm glad I'm not a teacher. I think I would go crazy. I would pick up Greg and his desk and his chair and drop them out the window. I'm not doing soccer. I'm sure not going anywhere that Greg is going.

Mr. Olson comes over to me. "So, Reeve. We're going to miss you at the dinner tonight. You can bring a neighbor if your mom can't come. It'll be fun."

"The dinner? Oh, the parent-child thing? Yeah, well, I'm-uh—busy."

"Going to sign up for soccer?"

"Soccer? Me? Nah. I don't think so."

"No? Why not?"

I shrug. I look down at my hands so he can't see my face.

He squeezes my shoulder. "Are you sure everything's okay?"

I nod. "Yep. Everything's fine."

When the 2:45 bell rings, my stomach drops like a high-speed elevator. I feel kind of sick, and my mouth is dry. Everyone's pushing and shoving out the door, yelling "Bye" to Mr. Olson.

Because of his behavior, Greg's on cleanup patrol. Mr. Olson has his arms wrapped around Greg's neck and is standing behind him, guiding him through the room to pick up bits of paper that are lying scattered about.

Mr. Olson's making it into a game. That way, Greg will do the cleanup but not get too angry about it.

Greg loves the attention. He's hollering out to everyone. Hey, maybe he'll be in such a good mood that nothing will happen outside. But I doubt it.

"Mr. O.," says Darryl, "how come you're helping him pick up?"

"Greg needs me," says Mr. Olson. "I'm his best friend in the whole world. Right, Greg?"

"No way!" Greg hollers, but he's smiling.

"Besides, Darryl, you know what? Sometimes I just get tired of being angry at kids. This afternoon, I'm feeling friendly, so you'll have to put up with it."

Mr. Olson throws one of his arms around Darryl, too, and gives me a big grin. I'm zipping up my book bag at a hundred miles per hour, which is also how fast I'm going to run out of this school.

"Isn't life wonderful?" Mr. Olson says. "Have I told you my wife and I are going to have a baby?"

"Yeah," says Darryl. "About fifty times."

"In a week or so. It's going to be a girl."

"Yeah," says Darryl. "We know."

Darryl smiles uneasily and glances at me in a kind of guilty way. He lifts Mr. Olson's arm off his shoulders. Then he looks down at the floor. "Greg, you missed a piece," he says, kicking a wad of paper out from under the heater with the toe of his sneaker.

"That's the last one! The floor looks great. Isn't that good enough? I gotta go, Mr. Olson," Greg says. "Please!"

"Gotta go? Where, if I may be so bold?"

"Umm. Well . . . home."

I can see Greg's getting nervous. He glances at me. Then I'm gone.

I nip out the door real fast and cruise by the kindergarten rooms to pick up Tasha. I keep looking over my shoulder. So far, so good. No one's following me. I may get off, after all. But Tasha's not quite ready, and by the time old slow-poke Tasha and I get out the back door, there they are—Greg, Darryl, and two other guys over by the fence. They've already got Brandon cornered, and they spot me the minute I step outside.

Uh-oh. Four on one. I can't believe it! This proves that Greg's a coward, but I guess cowards can be dangerous. Oh, my God. I don't know what to do. I wish I knew karate.

First, I have to get Tasha out of here. I grab her arm. "Listen," I say to Tasha. "Do what I tell you, okay? You have to walk home alone today. I'll catch up with you later. Just go down the hill past the bakery where the red trucks are, all right?"

"But why?"

"Just do it! I'll tell you later. Go!"

I give her a push. Ugh. The rocky lump that was in my throat at lunch drops down even deeper into my stomach. What if they go after Tasha?

"Tasha, go!" I yell. I shove her hard.

Suddenly she sees what's going on, and her stubbornness kicks in. She stands still with her biggest frown and doesn't move. By now, the four boys have come over. They surround me, Tasha, and Brandon and walk us out of the schoolyard. If you get caught fighting on school property, you can be suspended, that's why.

Brandon is pale as a ghost. His face is all sweaty. Mine probably is, too. I think things are going to get ugly. Now I'm really scared. What if one of them is carrying a knife?

Back at Auburn Street, lots of guys carry knives or pieces of chain or bent metal to hide in their fists in a fight. I don't have anything. What if they try to hurt Tasha? That's all I can think about.

Luckily, they don't seem to notice her. I stop walking just outside the fence. Oh, God, I hope no one has a gun.

"What's up?" I say to Greg. I can hear my voice sounding high-pitched and squeaky. I try to clear my throat, so he won't notice.

"What's up?" he yelps. "You know what's up, you creep. We don't allow snooty new kids telling us what to do around here. I don't know where you came from, but here you'll have to play by our rules."

Greg pulls and tugs at his T-shirt, kind of loosening up.

"Yeah," Darryl says. "We're going to teach you some rules."

Darryl has big front teeth that poke forward like a horse's. He's pretty scrawny. But what does that matter? Even if no one has a weapon, I'm in trouble. All Greg has to do is sit on me, and I'll be completely squashed.

Then, through my fear, I feel a surge of anger. This is stupid. This whole thing is stupid. "Well, I have a rule. It's don't pick on kids weaker than you," I say.

Greg steps in front of me and squares off. "You calling me a coward?" he asks.

"I'm getting a teacher!" Tasha yells. And she takes off. I see her little legs pumping hard as she races toward the school. I know it's all over for me. I know it's going to be quick and dirty. Because they're going to have to leave fast.

Greg thrusts his chest up against mine. "Well?" he says. "Are you?"

Then I shrug and say, "Maybe." And that's it. They're all over me and I go down. I feel my ear being ground into the dirt. Someone kicks my throat. They're sitting on me, kicking and punching. I writhe back and forth in the dirt, struggling to break loose. I can't even tell where I'm getting hit.

Then it's over. They all jump up and go running off, but not before Greg says, "Listen, trash lover, you tell on us and you're dead."

I sit up. My throat hurts something fierce. That and the side of my head by my ear hurt the most. I draw my knees up and rest my head on my crossed arms for a few minutes. My clothes are covered with dirt. I'm trembling all over. I wipe away my hidden tears.

Brandon kneels down. "Are you okay?"

"No!" I answer. "Leave me alone."

A teacher comes running over. She bends down. I can see the folds of her red dress where the hem lies on the gravel. I see Tasha's shoes and frilly white socks.

"Are you all right?" she asks. "Who was it? What happened? Can you tell me?"

I don't lift my head. "Nah."

"Do you feel ill?" she says.

"No, I'm okay. I'll get up in a minute."

She waits. But I don't move.

"Tasha?" she says. "Who did this?"

But Tasha doesn't answer.

"Who's your teacher?" she asks me.

"Mr. Olson," I mumble.

Tasha and Brandon don't say anything. The teacher stands there, hesitating for a minute, I guess not knowing what to do. The red dress reminds me of a teacher who used to come to the Auburn Street library, Miss Robinson. Miss Robinson was the best.

"Tasha, who did this? Can you tell me?"

"Some big kids. I don't know them."

"Boys?" she asks us. "Come on, now. What happened?"

We don't answer.

"I'll be fine. Really," I tell her. "It's okay."

The teacher gives a little sigh. "I'll speak to Mr. Olson and someone in the guidance office tomorrow morning," she says finally, and heads off to her car.

After I hear her drive away, I get up.

Brandon stands there, limp as a rag. They called me "trash lover" because he's white. I feel really angry with him. This is ninety percent his fault. He's a coward and Greg's a coward. Four kids on one. That's pathetic. And Brandon didn't even try to help.

"Get out of here! Quit staring," I say in a croaky voice. "Just go home."

Instead of leaving, he turns and runs back to the school, crying. Well, I can't help that. I guess he's afraid they may be waiting for him somewhere.

"Those guys are bad," Tasha says.

"Yeah, I know. And you know what? Mama wants me to play soccer with them this summer." I shake my head.

"She does?"

"Yeah. She wants me to be friends with them instead of Robert."

"Huh? I thought Robert was your best friend."

"He is. I guess . . . I mean not *instead* of Robert . . . She wants me to try to get along with them. I don't know. Never mind for now. I'll tell you later. Come on, Tasha. I got a headache. Let's get out of here."

I stand up and dust myself off. Mama hates fighting. She tells me that no matter what, I gotta walk away from it. One time last year, I got into a fight, a little one, and she went ballistic, yelling and screaming at me. It won't do any good to tell her I didn't start it. If she asks what happened to my clothes, I guess I'll have to tell her I slid into home plate.

Seven

We start down Cranston Street, toward the bakery. I have my hands in my pockets and I'm kicking a rock ahead of me. My throat still hurts a lot and my ribs, too. But mostly I'm shaken up. What if those guys come after me again?

I hate Greg. And Darryl, man, what a dweeb. After Mr. Olson was so nice to them, too.

Why didn't Brandon pick up those two tacks and march straight up to Darryl and Greg and tell them off right then?

Now I'm walking fast and angry, ahead of Tasha.

Tasha's saying, "Wait up, Junebug," and I'm saying, "Huh? I can't hear you."

But that's not true. Of course I can hear her. I'm just teasing, which is a new thing for me. I never once teased her when we lived in the Auburn Street projects. I took extra-good care of her there.

"You shouldn't have gone to get the teacher," I call out. "Now they're going to be really mad."

"What?" she asks, hurrying to catch me.

"Oh, never mind." I know how grouchy I sound.

I don't feel right, not since we moved. I don't feel right anywhere inside myself. If I were a snake, I'd probably be shedding my skin about now. For one month, our class had a snake when I was in third grade. One morning, I came in and there was the snake's old skin lying in the terrarium like a tube of crinkled wax paper—yellowish. Our teacher told us that's how snakes grow—their skin pops off. Now, that is cool.

I wish I were a snake right now. With a terrarium. I'd climb right inside and drape myself on a dead branch and watch everybody outside my tank with my drooped-over snake eyes. And I'd be saying with my snaky stare, "Leave me alone. Leave me alone forever."

Tasha and I pass the bakery on Cranston, turn onto Bellmore, then turn up the next side street, Robin Lane.

I say to Tasha, "Listen, you shouldn't have gone to get the teacher. Kids can get suspended for fighting, you know. Even if you didn't start it. Anyway, don't tell anyone else what happened today, all right? I'm fine, so don't tell Mama, cause she'll just be upset. I've had enough problems for today."

"Okay," Tasha says. "But what's suspended?"

"It's when you get kicked out of school for a while."

"Cause you did something bad?"

"Yeah. But I had to. Those guys had been picking on Brandon. Now, remember, don't tell Mama."

Then she says, "Your knee is scraped. And your elbow."

Whoa, she's right! Gotta get rid of the evidence.

"I can wash that gravel off. There's hardly any blood."

But Tasha won't stop talking, for once. "I hate those guys," she says. "They're bullies."

"Yeah, I hate 'em, too."

"But, Junebug, I should too get the teacher. Because my teacher tells our class, if big kids come up to you on the playground, go get help. So I did."

"Yeah? Well, okay. I guess so. That's what you should do, being in kindergarten," I say, changing my mind.

I give a big sigh. I need to relax. I want to be calmed down before I go into the apartment. The worst thing that could happen at this point would be for Mama to go boiling mad into the principal's office. Everyone would label me a tattletale. She'd ruin my reputation for life, and my name's already mud at King Elementary.

But I worry for nothing.

When we come inside, Mama doesn't even see us. She's sitting at the table in our dining area, staring at her patients' medicine charts. The past two weeks, she's always sitting there. Maybe she sleeps there. Tasha drops down on the sofa, steamed up from our walk home.

In the bathroom, I look at my scrapes in the mirror. I use toilet paper to clean off the dirt and blood and then toss the wads of paper in the toilet, so I can flush them away. Destroying the evidence. How did I get so sneaky? Probably from watching TV.

After I get cleaned up, I come out and take the rocking chair. When I rock fast, I can make my own breeze. I'm only a little shaky inside now.

"Hi, Junior. Hi, Tasha," Mama says without looking up. "I've got a licensing person coming to inspect my paperwork tomorrow, so hold on a minute. I just have to . . ." Her voice trails off.

Suddenly I notice a big rubber doll, life-size, like a store mannequin, leaning in the corner. Is Mama going crazy?

"Hey, Mama, what is that?"

Actually, it's only half a person, from the head to the waist. The legs and feet aren't included.

She doesn't answer.

"Mama?"

"Hmm?"

"That rubber doll in the corner. Is that a friend of yours?"

"Just a minute."

Oh, man, I hate living with Mama's job. Now we have to have this gigantic ugly old doll in the apartment. As far as I'm concerned, the doll is about the last straw.

"There," Mama says finally. Then she smiles at us. "I just had to finish the forms for the two new clients who came today. Mr. O'Sullivan and Mrs. Belinda Johnson. Mr. O'Sullivan is from Ireland. He wants us to call him Uncle Tim. And Belinda, she's a character! Wait till you meet her. She has seven grandchildren, and she has a separate photo album for each one. Plus she has an entire cookbook devoted to Jell-O recipes. She says Jell-O is her favorite food because of her delicate digestive tract."

Jell-O? Mrs. Johnson and her digestive tract? Uncle Tim from Ireland? We're filling up fast now. We already have Miss Williams and Reverend Ashford. Two more old people to go.

But photos? Help! Old people love their photo albums. If a photo album started coming at me, I'd jump up and run outside and scream. No, I wouldn't. I'm not going to be screaming today. My throat still hurts something fierce—a Popsicle might be a good idea.

I get up and head for the refrigerator. I don't want to look at pictures of old people's grandchildren.

Right now I wish I could be with Robert. I want to tell him what happened to me today. Four on one is so unfair! But if I telephone him, Mama might hear me talking about the fight. So I'd better not. I'll have to wait.

The open freezer lets a cloudy puff of cool air hit my face. I poke through all the Popsicles. Raspberry is my favorite, but the only ones left are watermelon. I grab one for me and one for Tasha and then go back to the rocking chair, sucking on cool ice.

Mama shuts the big folder she was working on. She stands up and stretches and rubs the back of her neck. Tasha runs over and throws her arms around Mama's legs. Mama bends to pick her up.

"Oooh," she says, slowly lifting Tasha. "You are getting way too big for this." She sets Tasha on the sofa.

"The tenants for the other two apartments aren't going to move in for a couple of weeks. The director of the nursing home thinks it would be better to give everyone time to get adjusted," she tells us. "So. Do you two have any school papers to show me?"

Tasha darts off to get her grade-one room assignment, while I think about the soccer sign-up sheet. I hid the parent-child dinner flier, but I figure I'd better show her this other paper. I'll just say I don't want to go. Simple as that.

"I got Miss Anderson for first grade," Tasha chants,

jumping up and down. She hands Mama her notice. "I got Miss Anderson. So did Ruthie. So did Ruthie."

Tasha has actually made some friends at the new school.

"Okay, okay," I say, going to my room for the soccer sheet. "We heard you."

What did Mama say? Time to get adjusted? Maybe that's what's wrong with me. I'm not adjusted. Somebody needs to fiddle with me as if I'm a busted motor or alarm clock. I'm buzzing and beeping and clunking at the wrong time.

Now Mama's reading the soccer sign-up sheet. Uh-oh. I'd better try to distract her. "Mama, for the last time, what is that thing in the corner?"

"Oh, that? That's a doll from the nursing home. For CPR training with mouth-to-mouth resuscitation. I have to practice on her for tomorrow. I'm taking a refresher course in CPR. Her name is Annie, and she's modeled after a beautiful young girl who drowned in a river in Paris, France."

Tasha heads right on over. "Hi, Annie. She wants a Popsicle," she says to me. "Give me your stick when you're done, Junebug, okay?"

I roll my eyes in disgust but hand over the Popsicle stick. Tasha's moving in on rubber Annie.

"You can be the principal at my school, okay, Annie? But only for today. The rest of the time, I'm principal. Come on. School meets on my bed."

Tasha grabs the big doll around the waist and lugs it into our bedroom. From the rocker, I see her sit it up against the wall and introduce her stuffed animals to it.

Jeezum. I cannot believe this.

Mama's still looking at the soccer paper.

Then I start thinking. Why does Mama need to know CPR or mouth-to-mouth or any of that stuff? The old people here, all of them are sick. But it's the kind of sickness people just live with. Miss Williams has diabetes and no kidney on one side, but she goes out jogging in her gold-and-purple track suit. Reverend Ashford walks slow and wears a hearing aid, but he's sturdy enough, except that there's something wrong with his breathing. When we walk, sometimes he stops to catch his breath. And he likes to sit down a lot.

"I thought you told us that if the residents got sick, they would go to the hospital," I say.

"Oh, they will. CPR is only for emergencies, until help arrives."

Mama looks at me then. "You know, it might be a good idea for you and Tasha to learn a little emergency care, as well."

"What for?" I frown. Now, hold on a minute. Don't I have my own life to live?

"So you can help out. Maybe you could think of this as our new family," Mama suggests.

What? This? A family? "No way!" I burst out, full of anger. "This is like living in a hospital."

The whole day has been too much! I start rocking fast.

Mama presses her lips tightly together. "You know, I'm not very impressed with the way you feel about elderly people."

"Well, I can't help it. They get on my nerves."

I regret it the minute I say it, but it's true. I can see I've hurt Mama. I'm afraid I'll burst into tears like a big baby. Although I know what she's saying is true, I don't want to hear about it today. That's all.

Mama pulls me from the rocking chair to the sofa and sits down next to me. "When you don't like somebody, you have to keep trying. You have to reach out to people," she says like a know-it-all Sunday-school teacher.

I can't see myself ever reaching out to nasty old Greg, that's for sure—or even to Brandon, for that matter. I shake my head.

"What?" Mama asks. "What are you shaking your head for? You do have to reach out to people. It's important."

"Oh, yeah? When you get mad at somebody, you don't do it. You haven't called Aunt Jolita once since we moved."

Aunt Jolita is Mama's younger sister. We used to live with her at Auburn Street, but she was hanging out with some real bad people who were into stealing and selling drugs. She and Mama had big fights.

"I told her I'll be glad to talk with her when she gets her act together," Mama said.

But I won't let up. "And you stopped calling Dad years ago because you don't want me growing up like him or even knowing him."

Suddenly I see Ron grinning at me in the sailboat, taking a friendly swipe at my head, telling me how well I'm doing. Tears jump to my eyes. I see Mr. Olson bending over me, asking me about the spaghetti dinner. I see Mama smiling at Walter, hardly knowing that I'm in the room.

I burst out. "I bet you didn't even give Dad our new address."

It's Mama's turn to be angry. "That's my decision. And I have a very good reason for it, as you well know. Now I'm asking you to show me respect. You will take this sheet to school tomorrow, because you're going to soccer this summer and that's final! Go to your room, Junior, until you've calmed down."

I don't want Mama to be angry at me. I want someone to be nice to me. I start to cry, run into the bedroom, and slam the door. I throw myself on my bed, sobbing into my pillow.

I know why she doesn't let us call my dad anymore. She worries to death that he might have a bad influence on me because he committed a crime. She wants me to grow up different from him. She got a divorce, to make the separation final and everything. That's okay for her, but what does it mean for me and Tasha to be different from him? I hardly remember what he looks like or the sound of his voice. Did he play football when he was young? What kind of music did he like? I don't even know.

With everything being so scary in the projects, Mama, Tasha, and I stuck close together. We had to help each other. Now it seems that every day each of us is moving apart, and there are all kinds of other people floating in and out of our lives. Mama has her new friend, that guy Walter, and her new job, and even Tasha has made friends already, with Miss Williams and with Ruthie at school.

But what about me? What am I supposed to do? Eat lunch with skinny-bean Brandon every day? Listen to guys call me names behind my back all the way through fifth grade? Make friends with the elderly? Today was awful, start to finish.

I miss so many things from Auburn Street—not the dirty lobby or the scary staircase, or the drug dealer we called Radar Man, who parked his Mercedes out front in the afternoons, but other things, like knowing Mama's friend, Harriet, was always just down the hall, or going to school with Robert. We were tight. Loyal. We all kept an eye out for one another.

A little later, Tasha tiptoes over and puts Theo, her

favorite teddy, by my pillow. I grab him and hug him, but I don't even say thank you.

Tasha stares at me for a minute. "I'm telling Mama what happened today."

"No! No, don't you dare. Come on, Tash. You promised."

Tasha gives me her big stubborn frown. "Okay, but what about tomorrow?"

"What about it?"

"What if they're waiting for you again?"

"Don't worry. They won't be. I can handle tomorrow."

I wish I believed it. Handle it? All by myself? Not likely. Not without a friend like Robert. Or some kind of magic power on my side.

Tasha shuts the door and goes away. I think about the bustle and sawdust and noise of the boatyard, and Ron's blue tattooed rose, and the soda machines everywhere. I see myself with Ron in the little gray boat, bailing it out with a cutoff Clorox bottle, taking off in the gusty wind, taking on the salty spray splashes, and hearing the cry of seagulls above.

I gotta give myself a smile and a pat on the back, because that stormy day I was brave for sure. And today I dug my heels in when I had to. Sooner or later, a guy has to do that. I don't think Mama would understand, but I think I did the right thing.

I'm still stirred up. I have to tell somebody what

happened. But who? I come out of my bedroom and go to the phone in Mama's room. I dial the boatyard.

"Hey, Ron? It's me, Reeve. Saturday's so far away, I wondered—can I come down tomorrow?"

"Well—sure. I might be busy, though."

"I don't mind. I can hang out. No problem."

Eight

The next day is Tuesday. School gets out Wednesday. Thank goodness for that.

I wake up with an extra dose of grouchy pills already in me. I want to leave early for school. I dread seeing those two guys, Darryl and Greg, but I also want to see them as soon as possible and get that part over with. I just have to get through today. Tomorrow will be a snap.

Nice and early, Mama pushes me and Reverend Ashford out the door. We stand there for a moment, taking in a new morning while it's still a little bit quiet and the air feels soft and fresh, as if it had been sleeping on a cushion of grass. The air above grass feels different from the air above tar.

"I had a bird feeder in my old yard," says Reverend

Ashford. "This time of year, the birds get up early. I used to like that."

I don't say too much about that. I never had a bird feeder. We lived on the ninth floor of a high-rise.

"So?" he asks. "Pretty quiet today, aren't you?"

I nod. I feel as if I have a padlock clamped on my mouth. There's only one thing I want to talk about, and if I can't talk about that, I'm stuck and can't talk about anything.

"Reverend Ashford," I say, "can you keep a secret?"

After all, I'm keeping a secret about him—his cigarettes—so I figure he owes me one.

"Maybe. How big a secret is it?"

"Medium-large to medium."

"Okay. Try me."

I take a deep breath. "Yesterday I got beat up at school. Four kids on one. It was so unfair."

We reach the bottom of Robin Lane and turn to head down Bellmore for the reverend's newspaper and cigarettes.

"See that little apartment window up there?" I say, pointing to the window above the car-repair shop. "The kid who lives there is named Brandon, and he's scrawny and afraid of everybody, and some kids pick on him and stuff, especially this one guy, Greg . . ."

"And so you, the new boy, were called upon to defend his honor," says Reverend Ashford.

"How did you know?" I say, surprised.

"It's an old, old story. But go on."

"Yeah, well, I can't tell my mom about the fight because she doesn't want me getting involved with stuff like that. But she wants me to sign up for this summer soccer team, and all the kids who beat me up are on the team! Not only that, she wants me to make friends with Brandon. And I can't. I swear. You know that kind of kid, sort of helpless? He gets on my nerves something fierce! I don't want to do the soccer team, but she's making me. And I don't think she should make me. I think she should let me go down to the boatyard and hang out. That's what I want to do."

"Huh," he grunts. "That's a long secret. Let me think about the first part first."

By this time, we're almost at the corner store. Reverend Ashford gives me a five-dollar bill for the cigarettes. I stand still and look at the money. I don't know if I should do this anymore, buy cigarettes.

But I don't give the money back to him. I just stand there waiting for him to decide. He snatches it angrily out of my hand, and then I feel bad. He marches into the store and comes out with a newspaper, a pack of Camels, and a roll of Life Savers for me.

"Hey, thanks." I peel it open and pull the little red string. On top is a green Life Saver. Supposed to be lime-flavored.

"Tell me what you do down at the boatyard," he says.

He lights a cigarette and coughs as he inhales. It would be good for him if there was a bench outside the corner store, but there isn't.

"Well, the manager, Ron, takes me sailing after he gets done with most of his work, and I help with just about everything. Only when I went on Sunday, when you and Walter drove me, he was real busy because everyone was putting their boats in. I want to go down this afternoon after school. I bet I could walk there if I had to."

"Well, the boatyard sounds like a good deal. So does soccer. There must be some decent kids on the team. The trick is to find out which ones without getting pounded too often by this guy Greg."

Reverend Ashford stops walking. Walking and talking at the same time is pretty hard for him. And we have to wait a while for him to catch his breath. Makes me remember that, for him, these walks are real hard work. No wonder he likes to sit home and watch game shows!

"Besides that, you don't want to put Ron in a tough spot and wear him out while he's on the job. So I'd say you have to find a way to do both. Compromise."

Compromise? Maybe. Neither one of us has much to say for a while. I'm sucking on that little green Life Saver. And we slow way down at the bottom of Robin Lane for him to rest again.

"Walter likes my mom," I say finally.

I stop walking as it hits me. I realize that that's

where my sharpest pain lies. It's not my sore ear or aching throat or bruised ribs. It's the thought that Walter's going to take my mom. Someday soon. I can't bear to think about someone barging into our family. Tears sting my eyes.

"So today's your worst day, right, with this fellow Greg?" says Reverend Ashford. "If you can get through today, you've got a short break before soccer starts. How about Walter comes to pick you up at school and drives you down to the boatyard?"

"Really? Do you think he would?"

I start to laugh, thinking about me and Tasha climbing into the blue truck, driving off, leaving Greg behind.

"He's never let me down. My son's the boss of his own company, young man," says Reverend Ashford proudly. "He sets his own hours. And you know someone you might talk to about your fight? Miss Williams."

"What? Miss Williams?"

"She came by for coffee while you were off at school yesterday. She's an amazing woman," he says softly. And I think I see a little flickery sparkle cross his face.

Hey! I wonder if old people can fall in love.

Reverend Ashford and I sit on the cement bench until we're allowed to go in. I hurry and grab my school things from my bed.

"Tasha, come on!" I call out from the doorway. "Mama, Reverend Ashford says it's okay for Walter to take me down to the boatyard after school. He can drive me there."

Mama comes out of the kitchen. She's holding the soccer sign-up sheet, and it's nearly all filled out! But not quite. If I hurry, I won't have to take it.

"Junior, quiet down. You'll wake everyone up. It's barely after seven-thirty. What's that about Walter?"

So I tell her again.

"The boatyard? I sure hope you aren't intruding on Ron's work time. Remember on Sunday how busy he was?"

"Yeah, but he won't be today. It's Tuesday. Middle of the week. Nobody will be there. Anyway, he said I could stop by. I got to get to school early. Look how slow Tasha is, Mama. She does it on purpose. I'm waiting outside."

"Good," says Mama. "You do that. You've got enough pent-up energy to light up half of New York City. Hey, wait a minute. Well, I guess you can take this soccer sheet tomorrow."

I head outside and go over to the little park. I stand on one of the benches. The morning air still smells clean and soft, not like yesterday. Hasn't filled up with car-exhaust fumes yet. All of a sudden, I see someone in a flashy bright gold-and-purple track suit turn the corner and come trotting up Robin Lane. It's Miss Williams.

"Hey!" I yell.

"Hi, Reeve."

She trots up to the bench and starts some slow stretching exercises. Puts her legs in a position so she looks as if she's riding a horse. "The horse stance," she says. Then smoothly she turns sideways and draws her right foot up on tiptoe. "The cat stance." And she does look just like a cat!

Miss Williams is a tiny person with feathery-soft light-brown skin and gray hair that is starting to turn white.

"Mama says you're sick," I say. "So how come you go out running?"

"I am sick. I have diabetes. All the more reason to get the blood flowing. But I'm late today. I like to get out really early. That's probably why you haven't seen me before. After I run, I go in and practice tai chi."

"You do what?" I burst out laughing and fall off the bench. The thought of this tiny old lady doing martial arts cracks me up. Too bad she wasn't with me yesterday for the fight at school.

"Tai chi. It's for balance and muscle control. It's wonderful. You should try it. I've started giving Tasha lessons."

"Yeah? Tasha? Tai chi's good for self-defense, isn't it?" That's what I want to know.

She twists her shoulders from one side to the other.

"What does a young gentleman like you need self-defense for?" she asks.

"I just do," I mumble.

And I need it quick. Like today.

"Let me see your arm for a minute. What's this scrape on your elbow? Your mother didn't put a Band-Aid on that?"

"No. I didn't show it to her."

Miss Williams looks at me thoughtfully. Finally, Tasha's coming down the walk.

"Well, we have to go now," I say.

"Reeve, you know you're welcome to stop by my apartment any time. I don't always have to drink tea with Tasha's teddy bears. I have time for you, too, you know. Stop over and I'll show you some tai chi, if you like. I'll even give you a private lesson."

I nod. Then Tasha and I head on up the street. Could Miss Williams really teach me some self-defense?

"Hey, Tash, you know that tai chi Miss Williams does? Is it easy to learn?"

"Yeah. It's got some blocks and stances and stuff. But mostly tai chi's about being a tree. A young tree." Tasha nods her head.

A tree? See, this can't be right. I should know better than to ask an almost-six-year-old.

When Tasha and I reach the playground, I tell her, "Listen, walk straight through everybody like we have to go to see your teacher. We're going in the kindergarten door to keep an appointment. Now hurry."

I catch a glimpse of Darryl and Greg in the group of older kids along the fence. Quickly Tasha and I weave our way through the crowded playground over to the side door and safely slip inside.

Nine

Brandon arrives late—after attendance—just as kids are handing over soccer sign-up sheets to Mr. Olson. When he gets to our row, Mr. Olson gives me an extra glance and wiggles his eyebrows to see if he can coax a soccer sheet from me.

"I didn't bring one in, Mr. O.," I mumble. "I—uh—I forgot."

Now I'm lying to my mother *and* my teacher. There's no excuse for that, and I know it.

"Stop by for a second during recess. I want to talk to you."

Uh-oh. The rocks are back in my stomach, but I nod. Greg's watching me like a hawk—I can feel it. He thinks everything that happens in the whole world is about him.

"And, Greg, you need to report to guidance before class. Be back by nine-fifteen for the math-assessment test."

"You mean go now?"

"Yes. Now."

Mr. Olson is glaring at him. I wonder if that teacher in the red dress told him about yesterday. Oh, God. My stomach is aching with dread.

Greg slumps out of the room, while Mr. Olson does some math review on the board to warm us up for the test. He always does that. He says kids do a lot better on tests when they're not nervous.

"You warm up for a race, right?" he says. "So why not for a test?

When the morning-recess bell rings, everybody pushes toward the door, extra noisy because the last day of school is so close. Mr. Olson tosses the playground ball to the girls. It's their turn to be team captains today, and everyone goes out. Mr. Olson pulls a chair over to his desk and points at it for me to sit.

"So, how's it been for you at a new school?"

I shrug, feeling kind of embarrassed. I guess by now he's seen me eating lunch all by myself.

"Okay, I guess."

"Really? Okay, I guess?" he asks. "If I had a quarter for every 'Okay, I guess' I've heard in the past ten years, I'd be a very rich man."

I smile.

"You know what 'Okay, I guess" really means in ten-year-old-boy language? It means 'Rotten'! Am I right?"

"Yeah."

I'm smiling, but I also have that lump in my throat again. I look at the chalky streaks on the blackboard. There's a portrait of Abraham Lincoln on the wall behind Mr. Olson's desk. Lincoln has a big, lumpy nose and sad eyes. He's Mr. Olson's hero.

"Have any big plans for the summer?"

"Yeah. I have a job . . ."

"Hey! That's great! Where?"

"I help out at the Fair Haven boatyard. But not every day."

"That's great. Going to be spending any time with your dad?"

I jump. I wasn't expecting this question. "Why? What do you mean?"

"Hey, Reeve, calm down, buddy. It's just that during the summer a lot of kids whose parents are divorced spend time with their other parent. That's all. You don't have to tell me about it."

My heart's pounding. I feel tears in the corners of my eyes. Suddenly I want to tell him about my dad. But when I glance at the clock, I see recess is almost over.

Mr. Olson leans forward. He says in a quiet voice,

"Did you know that you're keeping us all at a distance, Reeve? You don't have to be so strong, you know."

I shake my head. I reach for the Kleenex box. After I blot my tears, I carefully tear the Kleenex to shreds.

"So," he says briskly. "Want to know what you got on the end-of-the-year math test? That's actually why I called you up here."

"Sure. What?"

"You got one hundred. The only perfect score in the class. Before you came, the boys in this class looked up to Greg, trying to act out the way he does. Now, suddenly, there's a talented, handsome guy walking in and pulling hundreds, no sweat. You think maybe some of these boys are a little jealous of you?"

"No."

"Listen to me, Reeve. I've been teaching a long time. And kids who show true leadership skills, especially in the fifth, sixth, and seventh grades, kids like you, have a real hard time. A lot of the guys will criticize you, and you might not be the most popular boy in the class. But, underneath, they'll admire you. It's going to be hard."

Leadership? I start to laugh. He's got this all wrong! It sure doesn't sound like me he's talking about.

"Now I'm going to tell you something else. I'm teaching fifth grade next year instead of fourth. And I'm keeping you and a few others with me."

"Really? That's awesome!" Then I think for a minute. "Are you keeping Greg?"

"I sure am. Greg likes me so much I don't think he could live through a year without me."

I smile and shake my head.

"I'll tell you something else while I'm at it. Bullies are weak."

Quickly I look at his face. Of course he knows what happened yesterday. I guess that was why Greg had to go to guidance this morning. He'll probably take it out on me later.

"I admire you for being concerned about Brandon. Do me a favor, Reeve. Sign up for soccer. Stay involved. We need you. The world needs kids with leadership qualities."

Now I'm really laughing! Mr. Olson's crazy!

"Okay," I say. "I'll think about it." I don't want to hurt his feelings.

"Good. Now get your sorry butt outside. I have to get down to the teachers' room for half a gallon of coffee so I can face you ogres for another ninety minutes before lunch."

I run for the door. I wad the shredded Kleenex into a soggy ball. I take a fade-away shot at the wastebasket. McClain shoots! Off the boards. He scores, and the Celtics take the lead.

I get outside so late that recess isn't a problem, but lunch is pretty bad again. Same old stuff. All the guys are squashed in at Greg's table. Brandon's sitting alone. I start to sit down by myself. What the heck, I decide. I take my tray and go over and sit with Brandon. Maybe I can crack some jokes with him and get him to loosen up.

"Hey!" I say.

"Hi."

"You signing up for that soccer league?"

He shakes his head. I don't know why I even asked. I sit down and dive into my sandwich. Ham and cheese with a big dose of mustard and a soggy pickle. Cool.

"Hey, Brandon, listen. Next time somebody picks on you, like with those thumbtacks or anything, even name-calling, go right up to him and tell him off. You don't have to put up with that stuff. I know you're kind of little, but little kids can be tough. Don't put up with stuff like that!"

He doesn't say anything, just nods. I finish my sandwich, then peer into my bag. The carrot sticks are there, but no chips or cookies. I'm not on a diet, am I?

"Brandon. Want to do me a favor? Eat my carrots for me."

"Nah. I don't like carrots."

I glare at Brandon. He is annoying. The kid owes me a big, fat favor. I took on four kids for him, and he acts as if he doesn't even know it! He never even said thank you. You'd never know that he stood by and watched me get my face pounded into the dirt.

"Don't you care about anybody but yourself?"

He looks down and says nothing. Now I've hurt his feelings. Why did I say something mean?

After a minute, he says, "Why should I have to eat your carrots if I don't like them?"

I look at him, surprised.

"I wouldn't ask you to eat something you didn't like," he adds. "You told me to stick up for myself." He grins.

"Okay, okay. Sorry. Forget the carrots."

Man, this little guy is a mystery book from cover to cover.

Suddenly I see Greg toss his bag in the trash barrel and stroll in my direction. Uh-oh. A lunchroom fight? That would be suspension for sure. I put down my food and watch him every step of the way.

"You got me in trouble," he says.

"No, I didn't. You got yourself in trouble is more like it."

"I told you not to tell."

I don't want Greg to think about how Tasha went and got a teacher.

"If I get in one more fight," Greg says, "I'll get suspended immediately. And it's your fault."

"No, it isn't."

I lean back in my chair and look at him through

narrowed eyes. If he ever lays a finger on Tasha, I don't know what I'll do. I'll tear him apart.

"You're in trouble, man," he says.

Off he goes like Mr. Studmuffin.

"Get a life!" I yell after him.

Two girls are watching from the next table. As soon as he leaves, they come over.

"You're the first person to ever tell Greg where to get off," one, named Cassie, says. "I think it's great."

She smiles at me. So does her friend, Jessica.

"Thanks," I say.

Brandon has his head down. Well, he should. He wouldn't even back me up. Right about then, I nearly hate him. I don't know how I can ever be his friend.

Ten

The whole day at school goes by in a fuzzy, faraway kind of way. I'm not paying attention to much of anything. Then, in the afternoon, Mr. Olson has to go to one of those end-of-the-year meetings. Greg thinks the meeting is about him, because just before Mr. Olson leaves the room, Greg whispers to me, "What did he ask you at recess?"

For a second I don't answer him. Why should I? It's none of his business. But then I tell him.

"He asked about my summer job."

"And that's all?"

"And we went over my math test."

He looks surprised. Greg can't believe it, that anyone could ever have a conversation that wasn't all about him.

While Mr. Olson is gone, our class gets split up for

supervision. I'm in the group that heads next door with a map of America I have to put twenty-five labels on.

But I never get around to it. That's because I'm not even here anymore. Instead, Captain McClain is drifting far out to sea. I hear the seagulls cry overhead, and beautiful big white clouds roll and tumble across the sky.

It would be so cool if I could take my dad sailing. I see him sitting leaning back like Ron as we fly over the tropical waters, and he's smiling at me, telling me how well I'm doing. That would be great. I hope my dad's a lot like Ron.

Then I notice that Mr. Olson has come into the room and is making our class go back next door. On the way out, we have to hand him our maps.

Uh-oh! Guess I earned myself some homework.

Sure enough, after school, Tasha and I see Walter's blue truck parked across the street from the school, and we go running for it. It's great to climb into the cab and forget about Greg for a little while and leave school far behind. Walter drops Tasha off at Robin Lane and then takes me on down to the boatyard.

"So," he says. "School's almost over."

"Yep." I don't add anything else.

"I heard you've been taking my dad out for walks in the morning."

"Yeah, my mother makes us."

"A bit of walking helps him a lot, you know. But we just couldn't get him to do it when he lived alone. He'd stopped trying. You must have a magic touch. He must like you."

In spite of myself, I smile a little. But I can't think of anything to say. I've got nothing against Reverend Ashford now that I know him. It's pretty funny how he never tries to be polite; he just says what he thinks. I only wish my mother had never met Walter.

We cross under the Interstate and drive beside the train tracks that run along the edge of the Sound. There are sagging chain-link fences everywhere, lots full of barrels, oil-storage tanks, truck-delivery places. When we get to the boatyard, this time I remember to say thanks.

Walter turns off the motor. "Want to take a moment and show me around?" he asks. "Being a carpenter, I'd love to see the boatyard."

I don't know what to say. I don't want to show him around, and I don't want him to meet Ron, but twice now Walter's gone miles out of his way to drive me down here.

"Yeah, okay."

"Let's see that little boat you use."

"Are you sure you want to? It's way, way down at the end of the docks."

"No problem," says Walter. "Let's go."

As we head toward the docks, we have to pass the office.

"This is where Ron works," I say. "I gotta say hi."

I open the door. Ron's talking to some boat owners. I can tell because they're wearing those brown shoes with the white laces.

"Hey, Ron!"

"Hi there, Reeve. Be right with you."

By now, I know how much boat people like to talk to each other. So I know we have plenty of time to go down to the end of the dock. There's only a slight breeze today, and the dock is still. Walter follows me all the way out to the end.

There's the little boat, bobbing in the water. It's a soft, grayish, seagull color. Secretly, that's what I named it—*Seagull*. I know seagulls eat trash and stuff, but I love the way they hang in the air and soar in the wind.

"That's it," I say proudly. "I know how to put the sail up, and how to use the tiller, and everything."

"Well, that's great. I'm proud of you, Junebug."

Inside, I frown. He's got no right to be proud of me or Tasha. That's my mama's job, not his. Got no right to be calling me Junebug, either. That's a name for my family to use. And for my old buddy Robert.

"I better get going. Want me to pick you up around four-thirty?"

"Oh." I'd forgotten I'd need a ride home. "Uh, yeah. Sure. Thanks a lot."

"Okay. See you later."

Walter heads off up the dock, looking happy, and I stand at the end, looking grumpy. Now he gets to drive me home, and probably he'll want to stop in and see his dad, and then he'll want to come by and see Mama. It's just so easy for him to be around us. And there's nothing I can do to get rid of him.

Jealous. That's what it is. I guess I'm feeling jealous. I never felt truly jealous before, only little pieces of it around Tasha. It's a terrible, terrible sickly feeling. A worry sort of thing, feeling unsafe, not knowing what's going to happen.

There's only one way to cure myself. Take that boat out on the water! Come on, Ron. What's keeping you?

I start running up the dock. Ron's told me never, ever to run in a boatyard. But the water's calm today. The dock is pretty steady, not like Saturday. I'll be careful, I tell myself. I won't run fast.

My toe catches on a metal cleat that's fastened to the dock. I stumble once, my knees scrape the wood, and then I'm pitching forward into the cold water headfirst. My fingers scrabble at the canvas edges that line the dock, but I can't hold on. And I fall in.

Under I go. The shock of the cold water makes me gasp, and I swallow water. I open my eyes under water in a panic. Long wooden poles that support the dock stretch away from me down deep into the greenish water. And the depth of the water scares me. I start kicking and clawing my way to the surface. I know how to swim a little. I sure as heck am not going to die here. No way. I get my head above water and grab the edge of the dock, but it's too high for me to pull myself on to, so I hang there, shivering like a drowned rat. I cough and cough to get out the water I swallowed. It tastes terrible—salty and metal-flavored. I throw up a little.

"Help!" I yell. "Help!"

No one comes. Oh, man, it's cold.

"Help!" I holler.

I hear someone come running. It's a tall college-age kid. "What happened to you?" he asks as he kneels down to pull me out.

"I was running and I tripped."

"You're lucky you didn't hit your head on something. Listen, don't run around here, okay?"

The kid pulls me out. I'm standing on the dock, shivering.

"Wait a second. I'll go get a towel. Who are you with, anyway?"

"I'm with Ron. I help him out."

The kid laughs. "Some help you are. You scared me half to death."

He comes back in a moment with a towel and a gigantic sweatshirt.

"You want to get dry as soon as possible."

Someone must have gone for Ron because he comes hurrying along the dock toward me.

"Reeve, what's going on? You fell in, you crazy kid? Come on up to the office."

"Keep the sweatshirt for now," the kid says. "I can get it from Ron later."

"Thanks," I say as Ron ushers me away from the small crowd that's gathered.

When we get to the office, Ron slams the door hard behind me. I jump. He's really angry.

"You were running, weren't you?" he yells.

I never had a man yell at me before. It's scary.

"Yeah," I mumble.

He plugs in a little electric tea kettle and pulls a mug off a shelf. He takes a tea bag out of a little box.

"You know, Reeve, I don't know what you expect from me. But I can't watch you every minute. That should be pretty obvious by now. I think we'd better stick to Saturdays."

"Okay." I try not to cry. Now I remember that Ron didn't want me back until Saturday.

The tea kettle starts to wail, and he angrily yanks the plug out of the wall. He pours the hot water into the cup so fast it slops over the edge.

Then he sighs and pats my knee. "No, I'm sorry. I don't mean to be so hard on you. You scared me. Drink that tea down and we'll go out for a short sail. If you're too cold, we'll head straight back."

"Hooray!" I jump up, yelling, nearly spilling my tea. "Hooray! I won't be cold. I promise."

Ron shakes his head. "Drink up while I go get the sail bag."

Out on the water, we're scooting along. Not as fast as before, but it's still exciting. The quietness of it is exciting. Sailing, moving silently, magically. Just the sound of a faint ripple from the bow, parting the water's surface. Underneath us, the deep, deep, water wobbles away into darkness. And I saw it, the depth where the light vanishes, points in long rays into darkness.

Other boats are out sailing, too. We see two or three people on each one. The boats pass us, sometimes heeled over, and the guy steering gives a brief wave. And I realize I'll never know these people. Not their lives or what they think.

Before, when we lived at Auburn Street, my life was pretty simple. Keep calm. Lock the door quick. Don't make noise. Don't look at people wrong. I used to run my hands over the glossy turquoise photos of my sailing magazines. That was all.

But now everything is complicated, as if Tasha and Mama and I each got into our own boats and took off. Everybody's complicated—Brandon, Reverend Ashford. Something's bothering Brandon, making him sad, making Mr. Olson be extra nice to him. And it worries me that Reverend Ashford sneaks cigarettes. I wonder if they can hurt him.

And now Ron. I wanted him to be simple, too. I wanted him to be like a photo in my magazines. He could have been my dad, and we could have sailed to quiet coral coves far, far away. But now I fell in the water, and it's changed everything. Now he knows he's got a real live kid to keep an eye out for. And I don't think he wants to take care of me. I think maybe he already has his own life.

Eleven

Walter comes to get me right on time. There he is at four-thirty, parked right next to the rickety boardwalk and the office soda machine.

"Hey, kid," he says as I climb in. He sweeps his tool belt off the seat and onto the floor.

"Hi."

My clothes are still damp. But Walter was never a parent, so he doesn't seem to notice, and I'm glad for that.

"How was sailing?" he asks when I don't say anything.

"It was okay," I say in a small voice. "I'm getting pretty good at it. Just in the small boat, though. It doesn't have a jib sail."

Walter turns the truck around and we start bouncing along the rutted driveway back to the road.

"You don't need a jib to start with."

I look at him, puzzled. "How do you know?"

"Oh, it's just something I've heard."

"You know what? I tripped and fell in today."

"Oh, yeah?" He laughs. "I bet that water was cold."

"It was."

"Fall in in August next time. The water might be warmer."

I have to smile in spite of myself. Walter's good at making people relax.

We cross the railroad tracks and stop at a light. "Are you going to tell my mama?" I ask.

"Nope. No way. Are you?"

I sigh. "I don't know. Maybe not."

At home, I remember to thank Walter for the ride and I run inside. Quickly I get out of my soggy clothes and put them in the hamper. At least Walter had to go back to work and couldn't come up to see Mama.

Mama has Annie the CPR doll lying on the floor of the living room.

"Come on, Junior. Tasha, come on. Sit here, by me."

Mama sounds excited. She really wants to teach us a little resuscitation. But how much can a kid do to help a sick grownup? I'm not too excited about trying to revive the big rubber doll. It looks real, and it gives me the wicked willies.

"Is this CPR what you do when someone's drowned?" I ask, thinking of my fall into the water. "You really think Tasha and I could save someone?"

"You don't have to save anyone. But every second counts. If you know what to do before help arrives or how to get help yourself, that really matters. Anyway, you use CPR only on someone whose heart has stopped beating. CPR—cardiopulmonary resuscitation. It means restoring the heartbeat."

"Yeah, well, okay. Hold on a second. I have to eat something."

Mama's trying to get us to stop eating cookies. Now we have a big plastic container of carrot sticks in the refrigerator for snacks. I am a person who has always enjoyed a thick crunchy oatmeal cookie. I prowl around on a cookie hunt, just in case. Nope. No luck.

"All right," says Mama. "Let's get started. First, if you see someone's in trouble, you hurry over. Don't wait. Go right over and try talking to the person. You say, 'Can you hear me?' or 'Do you need help?' Then, if there's no answer, check to see if the person's breathing. Put your cheek down close to the mouth and look to see if the chest rises. If the person isn't breathing, you'll have to give a couple of breaths. Check for a pulse. I'll show you how later. Now's the time to send someone for help. At this point, you should know if the person needs just artificial respiration or that and CPR, too. If neither, keep talking. Even a person who seems unconscious might be able to hear you. Oh, and cover the person with a jacket if you have one."

Mama sits back, smiling. "There. That wasn't so bad, was it?"

Not so bad? I don't remember a word Mama said. Then she adds, "Tomorrow we'll do choking."

"You mean the Heimlich maneuver?" asks Tasha. "My teacher already taught us that. Stand up, Junebug. Mama, watch this!"

Tasha wraps her skinny, puny arms around my chest from the back and gives me a sharp squeeze. Oof! I didn't know she was so strong.

Oh, man. Tomorrow's the last day of school. We shouldn't have to learn anything right now. My brain's on overload. I may short-circuit at any moment. I flop back on the rug and stare at the ceiling. I flail my arms and legs.

"Revive me! Revive me!" I yell. "I'm dying."

"Okay," says Tasha. "Put your mouth up like Annie's."

"No way!" I roll over onto my stomach. "Mouth-to-mouth is disgusting."

"Not compared to the alternative, it isn't. Listen, get up," says Mama. "Harriet's coming over to play Scrabble. I made you guys tuna sandwiches and vegetable soup. And there's ice cream for dessert. Only, Junior, don't take too much, okay?"

Someone bangs on the door. Tasha and I usually race to see who will get there first. I open it. It's Harriet, Mama's best friend from Auburn Street, with her

Scrabble board and Miss Williams. In no time flat, the ladies have the board set up on our dining-room table. They're playing Scrabble and hooting and hollering. Harriet's got the dictionary out.

Tasha and I go off to the kitchen to get our supper while the ladies argue.

"I'm telling you, Rosalie, you are wrong. There is no such word as 'herf.' It even sounds bad." Harriet is whipping through the thin dictionary pages, muttering to herself. "You know perfectly well that you made this up, Rosalie."

"The word 'herf,' " says Miss Williams, "means to clear one's throat. To herf."

"You kids have any papers today?" Mama asks.

"No."

Tasha and I finish eating in about thirty seconds and put our paper plates in the trash. Then Tasha runs to get Theo from her bed to plop on Miss Williams's lap. And guess what I see on the kitchen counter? That yellow soccer paper all filled out and signed.

I'm trapped. Greg's going to get me at soccer. I know he will. My summer is ruined!

Mama gets up and comes into the little kitchen area while Miss Williams and Harriet are still arguing about the word. "This soccer program looks good, Junior. I don't understand why you don't want to do it."

Mama bought new Popsicles. I grab a raspberry one.

I edge past her in the narrow kitchen and go back to the living room, parking myself in the rocking chair. She follows me.

Mama doesn't believe in fighting, so I can't tell her four kids beat me up. And I can't tell her all the guys in my class hate me except for Brandon, and maybe he hates me, too, after today at lunch.

Mama looks annoyed. But she sits down and stares at her row of tiles. I see a word from where I'm sitting—"last." She also has a whole bunch of "i's." Instead of taking her turn, she dumps all her letters back and takes a new load on her rack.

She glances up at me. "You must have a reason you're not telling me."

I shake my head, but don't exactly answer.

Miss Williams makes a funny coughing sound.

"Is that supposed to be a 'herf'?" asks Harriet.

"It *is* a herf. Nothing supposed-to-be about it," Miss Williams answers.

I look over at rubber Annie, the doll, still leaning in the corner. I was hoping she would be gone today. Instead, there she is, and Tasha is feeding her a cup of pretend tea!

I don't stand a chance around here. While Mama's taking her turn, I go into her bedroom, gently close the door, and try to call Robert.

What a sneak! See? I never called Robert in secret before. Sometimes when I call him, though, the phone rings and a robot voice comes on. "This number has been disconnected." It means Robert's mom didn't pay her phone bill again.

I'm hoping the phone is fixed. Come on, phone! It's ringing.

"Robert!"

"Junebug! What's happening?" he asks.

"I don't know. Not much."

"How's school?" he says.

"I don't know. Pretty bad, mostly. My teacher, Mr. Olson, he's really nice, though. But listen to this. Yesterday, these four guys beat me up. Right in front of Tasha."

"Four guys! Where were you?"

"Just outside the school fence."

"Four guys? Four? Hey, that's not right."

"Yeah. You're not kidding. I got pounded pretty bad, especially in the throat."

"Are you scared?"

"This morning I was. But not now. I'm over it. The thing is, these kids are all in a soccer-league thing my mom is making me join. I keep telling her I don't want to. I told her you and I had a lot of plans for the summer."

"Course we do. I bet she was not too impressed with that."

"She wasn't."

"Hey, ask your mom if you can come sleep over tomorrow."

"I bet she won't let me."

"Yeah, well, ask her anyway."

"Okay."

I go out to the living room. "Mama, can I go to a sleepover at Robert's tomorrow?"

She looks up. "No."

But, lucky for me, Harriet butts in. "Come on, Rachel. Give him a chance to see his old friends."

"He needs to work on making some friends around here," Mama says shortly. "Invite Brandon over. Or someone else from your class."

Harriet makes a long face. "Well, well, well," she says, teasing Mama for being so strict. "Sorry, Junebug. I tried."

I go back and tell Robert I can't come. Then I go lie on my bed, discouraged. I don't know when I'll get a chance to see Robert again.

The grownups are folding up the Scrabble game. Harriet won, as usual, even though Miss Williams was right about "herf." And now Mama has to take Miss Williams's blood pressure with the squeeze bulb and the big Velcro cuff. While Mama pumps up the cuff, Harriet takes Annie from the corner and dances around the room with her, singing, "I Could Have Danced All Night."

"You're welcome to stay for our CPR class," Mama says when Harriet and the doll fall onto the sofa.

"I'd come every week if you got me a male doll instead of this female one," Harriet says.

"Who are you teaching CPR to?" Miss Williams asks in surprise.

"The kids."

"Really?"

"Just how to get started, a few little things. Although I think I might have gotten carried away."

"You know what?" Harriet says to Mama. "One day you may turn into a doctor. You love this, don't you?"

Mama gives a little smile and shakes her head. "Kind of late to become a doctor."

"You're twenty-eight years old, but you act like you already got one foot in the grave," Miss Williams says. She's spunky, all right. "What exactly do you plan to do with yourself for the next sixty years?"

Mama just laughs.

"Okay, now. What do you want me to bring to the barbecue?" Harriet asks, getting out pad and pencil.

"What barbecue?" Mama says.

"The one we're having this Sunday right here to celebrate you being at your new house."

"Oh, that one." Mama smiles. "Bring whatever you want. Surprise me."

Finally, Harriet and Miss Williams leave, but not until they get the whole menu for a barbecue figured out. As soon as they go, Mama scouts around and pounces on the soccer sheet. And she's heading straight for me like a bulldozer.

"Junior, this is perfect. Soccer four days a week. How about a three-week session?"

"I don't want to. Brandon isn't signed up." I sound as stubborn as Tasha even to my own ears.

"Well, what do you have in mind for the next eight weeks?"

"I had thought about sleeping in every day till noon. Eating marshmallows. Having Robert for a bunch of sleepovers. Our annual family trip to the amusement park. Couple of trips to the beach. My boatyard job on Saturdays. A pile of cartoons and videos to round things out. And that would be it."

"No, that will not be it."

The sleeping-till-noon part of my schedule had already been ruined by my early-morning walks with Reverend Ashford.

"Can't Robert come over?" I ask.

"Fine. Have Robert over. He can come—once in a while. After you spend some time with Brandon. And after soccer practice! It gets out at twelve. You'll have the whole afternoon to yourself."

"I've got my job."

"That leaves six other days free."

"I just don't want to go!" I yell in complete frustration.

"Why?"

I shrug. "Because . . . the kids here . . . I don't know."

She waits, but I won't say anything more.

"Junior, go to your room. Stay there until you can talk about this properly and respectfully. You've been awfully moody lately. I don't know what's gotten into you."

I make a dive for my bed and wrap my pillow tightly over my head. After a while, Mama comes in and sits on the edge of the bed. I roll over. At least I haven't been crying, for once.

"I'm going to insist that you go. Try it for just three weeks. You need to make some friends. You need something to do. You cannot sit around here moping."

"You mean something to do besides walk Reverend Ashford," I add.

She strokes my forehead. "Right. Besides that."

Mama's quiet for a minute. "I want you to be happy here. It's so much better than before, Junior. We couldn't stay in the projects forever. Miss Williams is so nice. Tasha loves her. Reverend Ashford and Walter are great. And I'm sure we're going to like Uncle Tim and Belinda. Please. Let's make this work out."

I hear what she's saying, but at the same time I remember Mr. Olson asking me about seeing my dad in the summer the way other kids do. I know she's trying her absolute hardest to give us a good life. But a new little part of me is growing inside. I say, "Why can't you let me decide what I want to do? I should be able to choose my own friends. Let me make my own mistakes."

Mama sighs. She stands up and leaves the room. I lie there, my heart as lumpy as pebbles.

Finally, I get up.

Tasha pushes open the door. "Come on," she says. "We're going someplace."

"Oh, yeah? Where? Another tea party?"

"Nope. Just come on."

She leads me across the hall and bangs on Miss Williams's door. I haven't really spent much time inside Miss Williams's apartment. Miss Williams lets us in. Immediately, Tasha takes off her sneakers and tells me to do the same.

Miss Williams has soft music playing. She has pale green curtains at the windows and lots of ferns and a little gold statue of a fat guy. She says the music is bamboo-flute music. The furniture is pushed back against the walls. Tasha goes right to the center of the room and stands with her hands at her sides. Miss Williams is facing her.

Slowly, slowly, like sleeping fish, they begin to move in smooth, flowing steps and gestures. Every motion is perfectly controlled, perfectly relaxed.

So this is tai chi.

I watch for a while. Then I stand next to Tasha and start to move with them. I feel relaxed. I feel as if I am swimming. Then I notice that Miss Williams is breathing in a certain way—slowly and deliberately. And I do that, too, and I start to feel better than I have in a long time. The tai-chi breathing makes me feel strong, and suddenly I feel very, very sorry for

Reverend Ashford. Not being able to breathe properly seems a terrible thing.

Later, we all sit on the rug.

"That sure didn't look like a real martial art," I say. I wonder how I could use it to defend myself against Greg.

"Oh, it is," Miss Williams says. "It is based on an ancient principle of restoring balance, of soft force, of redirecting energy. Think about this. You are a tree—"

"See? I told ya, Junebug," Tasha says. "You're a tree."

"And your feet are roots growing, rooting you to the ground. Your breathing is intentional. You protect yourself from being hurt by bending, by giving. You give with the force and float around it. You redirect the energy that's been aimed at you."

I look at her in disbelief.

"Think of this Chinese saying, then. 'The tree that bends the most is the hardest to break.' "

"What?" I still don't believe her.

She laughs. "Stand up."

She plants her feet and relaxes her arms. She's about five feet tall, barefoot, wearing this little pale-blue silk jacket sewn in swirling patterns.

"Hit me," she says.

I burst out laughing. "I can't hurt you!" I say. "Mama would kill me."

"I won't be hurt at all. It's you who will be hurt. Now, come on."

"Oh, man. I can't do that."

"Yes, you can. Then you'll believe me. Hit me!"

"Okay."

So I haul off and try to punch her shoulder. But she gives with me, at the same time putting one foot between mine, so that I lose my stance and my balance at the same time. In a split second, I am sitting on the floor with my legs splayed out in front of me.

"Whoa!"

What a day. Knocked flat by a little old lady. My whole life is turning upside down.

Twelve

Reverend Ashford is waiting outside for me next morning. Now, that's different! I run up to him and start leaping in the air.

"Hey! Reverend Ashford, this is it!" I yell. "The last day of school!"

"Congratulations. But by tomorrow you'll be bored," he says. "Your mother tells me you're going to be on the soccer team this summer."

He coughs after talking, and we have to stop walking for a moment while he catches his breath.

"Yeah," I say gloomily. "I guess."

Then I remember my tai-chi lesson. "You were right about Miss Williams. She studies martial arts. Has she ever flattened you?"

Reverend Ashford snorts with laughter. "Nope. Can't say that she has."

"Well, she decked me in about one second, so you better watch out."

"I can take care of myself. Gonna be another hot one," he says, glancing up at the sky. He wants to change the subject.

"We're going to have a barbecue this weekend to celebrate the opening of the home. You have to bring something."

"I'll bring paper cups."

"No way! I mean, bring something you make."

"How about newspaper hats?" he says.

"Well, yeah. That would be good. I was thinking more along the lines of chocolate cake."

"Sorry. You bring the cake. I deal only in paper goods."

By this time, we're lined up across from Brandon's.

"Just a second," I tell the Reverend. "Let me try something."

I know he has to be awake. I just have to make those floppy old curtains move. Make them shake and dance. Yeah! I cup my hands around my mouth. "Brandon!" I yell as loud as I can. "Brandon! Wake up!"

Then we stand and watch. Soon the curtains do move, and there's Brandon's scrawny little head poking out, looking like a chicken.

"See? There he is."

I wave.

He waves back. Then the curtains flop back into place.

"Timid little fellow, ain't he?" Reverend Ashford says.

"Yeah. And he won't eat my carrots, either. You know what happened yesterday? I fell into the water. I fell off the dock at the boatyard."

"Swallow any seawater?" he asks.

"Yeah. I sure did."

He laughs and shakes his head. Then he starts to cough. He bends over, and it looks as if it hurts him, but he hands me money anyway. I go in and buy his newspaper and cigarettes for him, while he rests outside. Now I feel guilty as heck when I hand them over.

"Are you feeling all right?" I ask.

"Fine. Fine." He flaps his hand at me. "Let's go."

At school, first thing, before I even sit down, I hand Mr. Olson my soccer sheet, which was tucked into my back pocket.

"All right!" crows Mr. Olson. "Look who signed up."

Then he does his own rap song, of which he is very proud, even though it's terrible. "Up high. Down low. Around the back, let's go. Give me five!"

The kids all boo. They love Mr. Olson.

I slap him five and slump into my seat.

We spend most of the morning cleaning up the room for Mr. Olson. We take down the faded construction paper from the bulletin boards, scattering silver staples all over the floor. We wash the blackboards repeatedly to get rid of the streaks of chalk. We stack all the textbooks on the shelves under the windows. Someone accidentally breaks a venetian blind, and it comes crashing down. All the usual stuff.

At ten-thirty, Mr. Olson passes out next year's room assignments. And everyone goes nuts, running around seeing who's going to be where. Then a bunch of girls leave and come back with a big bouquet of flowers because Mrs. Olson is about to have the baby any day now. We all know it's going to be a girl because of some tests they had done.

Then someone remembers that Mr. Olson had said he'd dance a jig on top of his desk if Greg could ever be quiet for twenty minutes. So Greg sits in a chair up front, facing the class. Someone sets the cake timer at the number 20. And the whole class sits down to watch. After ten minutes, Greg starts to squirm.

"Come on, Greg. You can do it!" Darryl yells. "Shut your eyes. Squeeze them shut. Don't give up."

Tick, tick, tick. The little timer cranks down the minutes. Eight minutes. Seven minutes.

Then Greg explodes. "Shoot. I can't do it! I can't."

"Okay, you tried," says Mr. Olson. "I'll dance on the desk, anyway. But I need a guard at each door in case the principal comes by."

Two kids rush for the doors. Mr. Olson climbs onto the top of his desk. He tucks his necktie into his shirt.

And, sure enough, he does a little tap dance up there! He's tapping away and swinging his arms just as the bell rings. School's out at last!

"See you next year!"

"See you at soccer, Mr. O."

Everyone's hugging him. Some girls are crying.

"Hey," he's saying, "I'll bring the baby to soccer. I promise."

A few moments later, Tasha, Brandon, and I are walking down the hill, past the bakery, to Bellmore Avenue. I can't believe what I'm thinking. I'm thinking school's over, and even though it wasn't great, I'm going to miss it.

This is Wednesday and soccer's on Monday. Only a few days away. My body still remembers the bruises I got from Greg and Darryl.

After supper, after the dishes are done, Tasha undresses her dolls and loads them into the bathtub. She wants to put Annie in, too. I like the idea, but Mama won't let her. Annie has to go back to the nursing home soon.

"Come on, Mama. We can pretend that Annie is drowning and we have to save her! Just like it happened in Paris, France," I say, taking Tasha's side.

"No. Annie is leaving tomorrow. Tasha, find something else to play with in the tub."

Mama takes a pencil and paper and sits down to plan the Sunday-night barbecue. Just as she starts making a list of foods, what she already has and what she has to buy, the doorbell rings. This time, Mama runs to answer it. She's faster than I am.

Sure enough, it's Walter, standing there smiling at her. "Hi, Rachel. I thought I'd stop by for a moment. I'm driving my dad over to his sister's for the evening."

"Come in. Would you like something to drink? Something cool?" Mama asks him. She's smiling, too.

They move right away to the table and sit down.

"Sure. I'm in no real hurry. Do you have iced tea?"

"Junior, would you bring Walter an iced tea?"

What does she think? That I'm a waiter at this little one-table restaurant? Well, I'm not. I dawdle my way into the kitchen and open the refrigerator. I pour the tea and add three ice cubes, then dawdle my way back to the table. Tasha's splashing around in the tub.

"So, you don't like baseball?" Walter asks me as though he suddenly remembered a conversation we were having earlier.

"Not much," I say shortly. It sounds pretty rude.

"Junior is really enjoying his experience at the boatyard. Thanks for driving him down, Walter." She gives me a you-better-say-thank-you-and-fast look.

"Yeah. Thanks a lot."

"I'd like to build a boat one day," Walter says. "A wooden one."

I smile at him, but not much. Then I realize that

this would be a very good time to tell Mama I want Robert to come over.

"Can Robert come to the barbecue and then sleep over?" I ask.

"What are you talking about? I thought you were going to invite Brandon. Walter, would you like to come to the cookout, too?"

"Do you like spare ribs in jalapeño sauce? Yeah? Then I'll be there all right. Actually, I stopped by to ask if you'd like to go out to dinner on Friday night. I have a friend who just opened a restaurant."

"How wonderful." Mama smiles a soft, wide smile.

Oh, no! What have I done? Walter and Brandon!

I decide to head out for some candy down at the corner store on Bellmore.

"Come right back," Mama calls out to me as I leave.

Brandon? Walter? Might as well invite Greg, too. I don't feel like coming right back. I'm in a fussy mood. I shut the door harder than usual. Bang!

Thirteen

Heading down Robin Lane, I try to cheer myself up. Maybe Brandon gets more lively when he's not at school. But then I think of the droopy curtains, and I doubt it. Whenever Robert and I sleep over, we watch old monster movies, the fake-looking kind. And we laugh for hours without stopping and eat a lot of junk food. I bet Brandon doesn't like doing any of that stuff.

I turn onto Bellmore Avenue. When I come to Brandon's block, I glance across the street to see if anything's going on. There's a fan in the window of Brandon's apartment. The garage door is open, and I can see a car up on the lift. A man in grease-stained coveralls is underneath, looking up into the engine and holding a clip-on light. I take a big breath, cross the street toward their driveway. Maybe Mama's right. If everyone else in the family is going to have new friends, then I have to at least give it a try. I grit my teeth.

What the heck, I tell myself. Maybe Brandon's a really nice kid. He's probably just a little shy—nothing wrong with that. Look at Tasha! Talk about shy! But at least Tasha's brave.

The driveway's lined with rusty engines, coils of chain, an oil drum or two, a pile of tires, an axle. It reminds me of the boatyard. Same engine smell. I like that. What a great front yard, and it's all paved, so there's no grass to cut. I give it the Junebug vote of approval.

"Hello!" I call out.

Brandon's dad peeks out from under the car. "Looks like I'll have to replace the whole transmission on this baby," he says. "So. What can I do for you?"

"I'm a friend of Brandon's from school. I just wondered if he was home."

Brandon's father wipes his hands on a rag. He looks kind of surprised. "I don't think Brandon ever told me about any friends."

"Well, actually, probably not. I came at the end of the year. My real name is Reeve, but my nickname is Junebug."

"Nice to meet you," his dad says. We shake hands.

I feel pretty embarrassed by now. If Brandon

doesn't stick his head out that screen door in one more minute, I may have to move on to the corner store fast.

"Well, Junebug, go on up. I'm sure Brandon will be really glad to see you."

I open the side door and head up a narrow flight of stairs. At the top is another door, closed. I knock, but no one answers. I can hear the TV on, so I push the door open and go in. I go through the tiny kitchen to the front room, their living room.

Brandon's sitting on the couch, staring at a big-screen TV, watching cartoons, the complicated cartoons with sorcerers and guys with secret powers. I stand in the doorway. It's very hot up here. The floppy curtains in the living room are sucked up flat against the window fan. There's a table with two chairs next to me against the wall and a painting of a snow-capped mountain and fall trees over the sofa.

"Hi," I say.

Brandon jumps a mile, as if he's been shot. Guess he didn't hear me come in. Some kids get in a sort of trance when they watch TV, and I figure he's one of them.

"Hi," he says. Then he flicks off the sound with the remote, but he doesn't get up or anything. Finally, he says, "What do you want?"

"Nothing. I just came by to say hi." Man, this is hard work.

"Oh." Brandon thinks for a minute. "Want to see my room?"

"Sure."

He gets up and pads past me in his narrow bare feet. I follow him through the kitchen into a small bedroom off the back. There's not much to it. A saggy bed with a frayed pink blanket. A poster of a kitten that's half fallen down. And a chair with a chessboard on it, the pieces all set up.

"Want to play me?" he asks. "I'm pretty good."

"Chess? I don't know how. You got any other games?"

He shrugs. "Monopoly. Checkers—but that's for babies."

"Yeah, well, I'm a big fat baby, then," I say.

Brandon smiles. Finally!

"I'm sorry about the thumbtack thing at school," I say.

He nods.

"But you should have stood up to those two guys right at the beginning! What's wrong with you, man?"

"I'm sorry you got beat up," he says softly. "I'm sorry I didn't eat your carrots."

"Yeah, me, too. Hey, where's your mom?" I ask.

"She's sick," he says.

That makes me a little nervous. Maybe Brandon's sick, too, and that's why he's so weak.

"Is it something contagious?" I ask.

"No."

"Is she here? Is she sleeping?"

Junebug, I ask myself, why don't you ever learn? But I have to find out.

"She's in the hospital for a while. That's why I was a little late coming to school the past couple of weeks. We go visit her early. She's got cancer, and the medicine makes her really sick."

Brandon looks as if he's going to cry again. Some friend I am.

"Hey, you know what?" I say quickly. "My mother was in the hospital once when she broke her foot. She came home in about a week. I bet your mom will be home soon."

"Yeah? You think so?"

"Sure. Hey! What's this stuff?"

Sitting on a plastic tablecloth spread out on the floor is a plastic wastebasket and lots of small wires, circuits, batteries, and wheels.

"My dad and I are building a robot. The wastebasket is his body."

"You mean a real robot that moves around and brings you food?"

"Yeah. A real one."

He gives his little butterfly of a smile.

"Wow. You know how to do this?"

"Not really. My dad does most of it for me."

I step over closer to get a better look. "What's this piece—" I start to ask.

"Be careful!"

I hear a small crack under my foot. Uh-oh. "What happened?" I ask.

Brandon crouches down to take a look. "You broke a couple of circuits we glued together last night."

"Oh. Sorry. I didn't mean to."

Brandon nods again and sits down on the bed.

"I have to go. Come on over to my house Sunday around five. We're having a barbecue. My mom invited you. And your dad."

"Yeah? Okay."

"If your mom's home by then, bring her, too."

"Probably that wouldn't work."

"Oh." Then I don't know what to say. "Well, bye."

He doesn't say goodbye.

Even so, as I'm heading home with three Tootsie Roll pops in my pocket and a fourth one stuck in my cheek, I feel a lot better, kind of cheerful. Maybe I'm finally getting the hang of this neighborhood a little. Maybe it's time for me to take charge.

Back at the little park, Reverend Ashford is sitting on the bench where Tasha feeds her dolls. Walter's blue pickup truck, loaded with tools and ladders, is still parked in front of our house.

"Hey! Reverend Ashford!" I yell.

He spots me coming up the street. I run over and sit down next to him. I'd offer him a lollipop, but I don't know if he's got the teeth for it. That gooey chocolate center is powerful. It locks onto your teeth as if it's never going to let go.

"You want one?" I hold out the three lollipops. I hope he leaves me the orange and the red one.

"Don't mind if I do," he says. He takes the purple one and unwraps it. "So. No more days at school, right?"

Now we're both talking through our lollipops.

"Nope. Today. That was it."

We sit together, eating the candy. The sky is a hazy pink where the sun is going to set. The trucks are already parked, so there's almost no traffic on Bellmore and we don't have to talk over the tire noise.

"I had a porch at my house. On a shady street. Maple trees all up and down the street," he says. "It was nice to sit out in the evenings."

"Walter's taking a long time," I say. "Visiting Mama."

"He certainly is. We were supposed to go over to my sister Stella's for the evening. Don't know if we'll ever get there at this rate."

I want to think of a way to encourage Reverend Ashford to get Walter to stop coming over. "I bet Walter's got loads of girlfriends. He's probably real busy."

Reverend Ashford looks at me sideways. "No. Walter's always been shy that way with women."

Shy? I don't think so. He's barging into my house, practically taking the whole place over. That's not shy to me! Now, you take Brandon or Tasha—that's shy.

"So you think he's got a crush on your mama?" the Reverend asks.

"I guess." I know I'm scowling.

"What's wrong with that?"

I can tell he's trying not to smile. Grownups don't fool me. "Nothing."

"Huh. If you say so. What's your face all crunched up for, then? Don't forget our walk tomorrow, will you, just because you don't have school."

He coughs suddenly. After the cough, he looks tired.

"I won't. Anyway, Mama won't let me."

We sit quietly. Then I say, "My dad, my real dad, is in prison."

"That's hard," he says.

"Yeah. I guess. Reverend Ashford, does Mama really know you're smoking?" I ask.

"Of course she does. What? You think I'm sneaking smokes like a little kid? Listen, go on over to Walter's truck and give a blast on the horn. We're a half hour late already. If we don't go soon, I'm going to go to bed."

"Okay."

He does look pretty tired.

I trot over and lean in the window. I push the horn down for one long blast as loud as a ferryboat whistle. If Walter can't hear that, he must be deaf. Mama comes running to the door to see what's going on.

"Junior! Did you do that?"

"Uh, yeah."

"It's all right. It's all right. I told him to," says Reverend Ashford.

Walter takes Mama's hand and holds it for a second as he walks out the door. "Bye, Rachel. I'll pick you up on Friday, then." He gives her a quick kiss on the cheek. And then he and the Reverend drive off.

So Walter and Mama are going out on a date, and neither one of them asked my permission.

Fourteen

Friday night isn't too bad, though. Miss Williams comes over, and we watch a movie and then do some tai chi. Tasha says she doesn't want to be a ballerina anymore; she wants to do martial arts, instead.

Saturday I'm flopped out on the sofa, my arm dragging on the floor. Bored with waiting. Harriet's going to pick me up and drop me off at the boatyard, then go shopping with Mama for the barbecue. I wish she would hurry up and get here.

"Come on, Harriet," I groan.

I'm not doing too well now. I feel like a caged-up tiger, I'm so full of impatience. I flip onto my back and let out a big growl.

"What is your problem?" Mama asks. But she knows what's wrong and doesn't expect an answer.

I'm driving her nuts. I know. I'm driving myself nuts, too. On her bed, Tasha's got her dolls lined up, playing school. Tasha, of course, is the principal now that Annie is gone. She runs a tight ship. Her dolls don't stand a chance.

"You better get ready to go down to the boatyard, Tasha. Because Harriet will be here any minute. Go get your sneakers on, so we don't have to wait," I call out from the sofa.

"I'm not going," she says.

Now, what is this? Of course she is. She's only going on six, for Pete's sake. She can't stay here alone. Suddenly I hear a knock.

I jump up, yelling for Mama and Tasha to hurry. Mama grabs her jacket and purse, while I unlock and open the door.

"This child's about ready to jump out of his skin," she says to Harriet.

"I noticed," Harriet says.

Then Tasha comes out of her room, all loaded down. She's got two teddies under one arm, Theo and somebody else, and a whole stack of plastic dishes in the other hand.

"You can't bring all this in the car!" I yelp. We're going to be late.

"She's not going in the car," Mama says.

Tasha walks right by us and sets her teddies on the floor. She knocks at apartment 4-A. The door opens; Miss Williams smiles at her.

Tasha looks back at me. "Bye, bye, Junebug," she says.

Then she drags her dishes and teddy bears inside 4-A and shuts the door. Boy, Tasha is really changing. At Auburn Street, Tasha never visited anybody by herself. I had to take her everywhere.

"How come she's not coming to the boatyard?" I ask.

"Tasha's made other plans," says Mama, cool as anything.

"Well, I'll be," Harriet says. She can't believe it, either.

Then I'm outside and halfway down the walk to the car. "Let's go!" I yell out. Behind me, Mama and Harriet are laughing.

When I finally get to the boatyard office, I find Ron talking on the phone. He waves a big hello and gives me seventy-five cents for the soda machine. One thing I've learned about people who work with boats is that they drink more soda than you'd think could fit inside their bodies. There's a recycling box next to the soda machine, and it's always filled to overflowing. I get myself a Pepsi and pop it open. Ron covers the receiver with his hand.

"Listen, Reeve, I'm going to be on the phone for a little while. Why don't you wander around and come on back here in twenty minutes, okay? And don't fall in this time."

"I won't."

I head down the bumpy dirt driveway. To my left is a huge crane with a canvas strap. A big sailboat is being hoisted into the air with the canvas strap underneath. Two guys are on either side, yelling directions to the guy driving the crane. He guides the crane down some short tracks and into the water. When he lowers the sling, the boat floats free.

I head down the ramp onto the floating dock and walk carefully to the end. I'm still not used to the tipping feeling under my feet. After so many years on dry land, what can I expect?

Out at the end, the breeze is strong and fresh on my face. I sit down out there and drink my soda. Overhead, the clouds are big and white, pressing together like huge lumps of ice cream, then pulling apart. Two seagulls land on the dock's edge and watch me drink my soda. I pour some soda onto the planks, but they don't drink it. A fuzzy yellow-and-black bumblebee does, though. His black skinny arms have snags on them. He sticks his arms again and again into the soda, tanking up. He's going to get so loaded down he may not be able to fly home.

It's peaceful out here. The noise of the boatyard is behind me. I let dreamy thoughts weave through my mind. I could come out here every day and never get tired of it. My eyes are relaxing, half closed.

Suddenly I'm looking at two paint-spattered canvas sneakers. I have to laugh when I see those. "Hey,

Ron. You have the coolest sneakers. Every color in the world is speckled all over them."

Ron looks down at them. "I'm glad you think so. My wife won't let me wear them in the house. When I go home, I have to leave them here. So, you ready?"

"Ready?" I guess so. What does he have in mind for today? Barnacles?

"I have a big job that's got to be finished this afternoon, and it goes a lot faster with two people. I need some help putting out the new markers on the moorings."

"What are moorings?"

"The boats that aren't tied up at the dock are anchored to cement moorings in the harbor. I just got in some bright pink marker flags. I need to replace the old flags with them. But the guy who was going to help me couldn't come this afternoon, so it's a good thing you're here. Think you can help me out, instead?"

"Sure. Let's go." I jump to my feet.

We start back along the dock. Ron calls over his shoulder, "You can drive the launch. I'll do the leaning over the edge. I don't think your mother would appreciate it if you took another swim in the harbor."

Especially since I didn't tell her about the first time. Well, how could I? Mama's friends were over playing Scrabble, and I had soccer on my mind at the time. Besides, I told Walter and he seemed cool about it.

Now I have to drive the launch? I don't even know for sure what it is. Guess I'll find out soon enough. Ron hasn't let me down yet—except that he's a lot busier than I thought he would be. I guess all grownups are busy, except the older ones like Reverend Ashford. But that can't be true, because Walter finds time to bring me down here.

Tied up by the smelly old gas pumps is a large open boat with a blunt front. In the back is a pile of pink plastic flags on Styrofoam floats. This must be the place.

The boat has a steering wheel and a captain's chair. And I'm going to drive this thing?

I climb on board. Ron starts the engine. It chugs smoothly, vibrating the floorboards under our feet. I wish I had canvas sneakers like Ron's instead of big, clunky basketball shoes. While I strap on my life vest, Ron scrambles over some gear up front and unties the ropes. Then he puts his heavy hands over mine on the wheel and puts the throttle in reverse.

"Sorry," he says, "but backing out's a little tricky. Okay. Now you help get us out of here."

I keep the engine running at its lowest speed. We pass the long row of tie-ups and move carefully out into the area where the moorings are. Waves push in rows into the harbor. The anchored boats rock over them like horses nodding nice and slow. The steering wheel feels smooth under my hands.

"Think you've got the feel of things?"

I nod. Holy moly.

"Just keep the speed way down and do exactly what I tell you. We're going to pull alongside the old mooring flags. Then I'll take the boat hook and pull up the mooring chain. While I'm attaching the new flag, you idle the engine. Nothing to it."

Yes, there is. As usual, I have a question. "Since I'm sitting in the chair and doing the driving, am I the captain?"

"I'd say so."

Ha!

Captain McClain holds the chrome steering wheel and very gently turns left. He lets the engine idle while first mate Ron pulls up the first mooring. Then he lets the launch creep forward toward the next mooring. These are mines left over from World War II. If the crew doesn't get the mines cleared by this afternoon, there's no telling what the future of New Haven will be. A nuclear sub is due in from Great Britain. It has top-level secret documents on board. The harbor must be cleared, and McClain is the man to do it.

Slowly and carefully, McClain and his crew move from mooring to mooring, until each one is clearly marked with a fresh pink flag.

"All right," Ron says finally, straightening up. "Oof. My aching back. Let's take a little break. You can run us out for a spin. Mind if I use the chair?"

I hop off the seat and head for the open seas.

"Open that throttle up, kid. This launch has a powerful engine."

The engine roars, and the front of the launch lifts clear of the water. We're skimming over the surface; our bow is spanking the waves flat. The wind blows my breath away. I'm laughing with excitement. This is fun! Sailing is fun, too, but you have to think a lot—what you need to do next, where the wind is, how to steer and hold the boom rope at the same time. Compared to sailing, this is easy.

"How fast are we going?" I yell over the roar of the engine.

"Oh, close to twenty miles per hour."

"That's all? How come it feels like two hundred?"

"Twenty is fast for a boat."

We cruise out to a little mound of rocks like a tiny island that hasn't had time to get dirt on it yet. Ron tells me to cut the engine to idle. We sit quietly and drift in the waves, resting. I like how relaxed Ron is.

"Were you in the army?" I ask.

"Navy," he says. "I was on a submarine based in New London. You know where New London is?"

"No."

"It's not far from here. I got this tattoo in the navy."

"Do you have kids my age?" I ask, already a little bit jealous in case he does.

"I have a son, grown up now. I don't see him much.

He's in California. When your kids leave home, that's when you feel how big this country truly is."

"How come he left?"

"He didn't agree with some of the rules his mother and I had in our house. One day, he just left. We didn't hear from him for over a year. That was a sad time for us." Ron gives a little smile and rubs my head.

Why would a son ever leave his dad? I think Ron's son must have been crazy.

"I was pretty hard on him, I guess. I've tried to change since then. I've had some things I had to work out."

"Like what things?" I know I should stop asking questions. I promise myself this is the last one.

"Oh, things about alcohol. My son was pretty angry about that. He was right, too."

"You're not drunk now."

"No."

"So why doesn't he come back?"

"He's started a life somewhere else. I guess that's the main reason."

I lean over the side and trail my hand in the water, making swirls and whirlpools and looking at the colors. The water isn't just blue, as I'd always thought. It can be golden with sunlight streaks in it. It can be gray and foamy green. Right on the surface it looks blue until a cloud passes overhead. Then it shivers and turns gray.

"Hey!" I yell.

"What?" Ron has his feet propped up on the rail, eyes closed. He opens his eyes.

"Is the ocean blue because the sky is blue?"

"Yeah, I think so."

I want to ask why the sky is blue, but that's exactly the kind of question that puts grownups in a grumpy mood and they tell you to go look in the dictionary or something. Still, being me, I have to ask. "Ron, why is the sky blue?"

He keeps his eyes closed. "I have no idea. But I'm glad it's not purple."

"Sometimes it is. And pink, too. And orange. But not green."

"No."

"So how come the sky's not green? Why is it every color except green?"

"I don't know."

"Would the ocean be green if there were a lot of trees near it?"

"Maybe."

"You think God hates green?" I ask.

Ron bursts out laughing. "You better ask him."

God probably doesn't hate green. Maybe he just thinks he used too much of it when he made the grass and trees and stuff. When he got to the sky, it was time for something else.

I start thinking about Ron being someone's dad.

Since his son is gone, that can help me pretend he's my dad.

"I wish I could bring my dad out here," I say finally.

"Oh. Well, sure. Bring him along. Bring him down next Saturday," Ron says.

I don't answer at first. "I can't. He's in jail, actually. Well, not jail. Prison."

"Oh, yeah? You ever see him?"

"Nope. Not since just before Tasha was born. But I don't remember him very well. I was too little."

Ron shakes his head. "You know, you're a really great kid. And I can't imagine a dad who'd walk away and leave you behind. But I gotta tell you, Reeve, I'm not perfect, not by a long shot. That's what this is here for." He points to the rose.

"It's there because of your mistakes?"

"Yeah. I had it done when I was drunk. It was a long, long time ago. Listen, Reeve, I drink—well, I used to, and it's been hard for me to stop. Sometimes I don't act the way I should toward people I care about. So if we're gonna keep up this sailing thing, I figured you better know about that."

"Oh, it's not a problem," I assure him. "Really, Ron. Anyway, there's lots and lots of soda around. You can drink that."

He swats me lightly in the head and smiles. "Thanks."

Now I lean back like Ron and let the boat rock me.

My arms are warm from the sun. I like my brown skin. I like the way it looks next to the white sleeve of my T-shirt. I like looking at Mama's arms, too. I think about Brandon in his little apartment over the garage and how he's not really white. He's more sort of faded into no color at all.

Fifteen

At seven o'clock Sunday morning, I'm out front on the cement bench. It's nice and quiet—no vans or trucks whirring past on Bellmore Avenue. Mama's already up, too, and in the kitchen, cooking. She and Harriet love picnics with a passion. Mama's hoping to get her driver's license as soon as she has time to practice, so we can go on lots of them. For now, we have to stick with a backyard barbecue. Nothing wrong with that—except Robert's not coming, only Brandon. I feel bad about that.

Reverend Ashford shows up right on time. I knew he would. He and Walter both keep an eye on the time, but not in a hurried way. In a reliable way. I run over to him.

"Howdy, partner," he says. Two words, then a big breath.

"Hi! Are you still just bringing paper goods to the party?"

"Paper hats."

Those two words take all his breath. He holds still.

"Want to sit on the bench?" I ask. I'm getting real used to his lungs.

He nods. We go over and sit down.

"Want me to run down to the store and get the paper?"

He glares at me. "I'll come."

He stands up. Then he shakes his head and sits down. He reaches into his pocket and gives me money for the paper and an extra quarter for a gumball from the machine by the door.

"Hey, no cigarette money?" I ask.

"Not today."

"Okay. I'll be right back."

I run my fastest down Bellmore. My legs feel long and my sneakers feel as if they're flying. The air is clean and fresh. I feel light and fast, out running early in the morning.

When I get back, the Reverend takes the entire business section and folds it into a triangular Napoleon hat and sets it on my head. He salutes me.

After we do our reading, I help him back inside and I walk him all the way to his apartment. I want to tell Mama about how tired he was today, but the minute I get back inside, she's got me peeling a cucumber, and I'm not too good at it. I gouge and scrape, and I end up with a grimy little sorry stub of a cucumber. And when I show it to Mama, she says, "Oh, for heaven's sake. How could you do that to a vegetable?"

Seems like the vegetables have more rights than I do. Frying a ton of chicken always makes her stressed out. After I destroy the cucumber, I run down the hall to check on Reverend Ashford. Uncle Tim's in his room with him, and they're having a good time now, making all the paper hats for later. Uncle Tim is nearly totally bald and has foxy red eyebrows. They invite me to come in and help, but I have to go back and help Mama.

The picnic's all set for five o'clock. You'd think Mama couldn't make enough food. Mama doesn't trust chicken to get cooked enough on the grill, so we're just going to barbecue the ribs and the hot dogs. Miss Williams is making corn bread and brownies.

Mrs. Belinda Johnson is making a Jell-O salad. Her apartment is right next door to Miss Williams's apartment. I've been steering clear of Mrs. Johnson. She always has gas pains, for one thing, and she keeps jars of Maalox all over the place. Besides that, she's the one with the seven photo albums. And she spends half her life on the telephone, telling her grownup children what to do. At least, this is what I heard Mama tell Harriet.

Salad. I don't know much about it, but lettuce and

Jell-O don't sound like a good combination to me. I don't like potato salad, either, and neither does Tasha. Thank goodness no one is bringing that.

Reverend Ashford is bringing cups and plates. And Uncle Tim is bringing lemonade.

Harriet arrives with the charcoal, and Brandon comes next. Right away, Mama puts Brandon and me to work, lugging chairs out into the backyard. Then, together, we bring out a table to put the picnic stuff on. I don't think Brandon's ever had to carry anything in his life. Afterward we take a break and lie on the soft new grass.

I watch Mrs. Johnson come out with the salad. She's carrying it on a flat plate up high, as if she's holding a little fat king, and the shaking red Jell-O forms a dome shape, with grapes and pieces of other fruit floating like jewels in it.

Every time Mama bustles out of the kitchen into the yard, she looks around, probably to see if Walter is here yet.

Suddenly, around the corner comes Brandon's dad. Mama hurries over to greet him. He's brought a bag of chips and dip that comes in a foil cup.

At first, Brandon goes and stands with his dad. Then his dad gives him a little push and he comes back, embarrassed, and sits down with me and Tasha. Nobody knows what to say. We all feel pretty awkward.

Finally, Brandon says, "How does that lady, Mrs. Johnson, get the Jell-O to stand up like that?"

"You put less water in it," Tasha says.

She's getting pretty smart for a little kid.

"Tasha's going into first grade," I tell Brandon. But he doesn't say anything, and that gets on my nerves. He should respect Tasha. She's braver than he is.

There's definitely something wrong with his manners. He doesn't feel that he has to answer people. Maybe because his mom is sick and he's an only kid. I bet he never does any chores.

"It's nice here," Brandon says then, looking around at our yard. He pats the grass. "Very nice."

Reverend Ashford comes out, carrying the cups. He's wearing his suspenders over a white T-shirt, with his usual tan pants. He's wearing one of those paper Napoleon hats.

"Hey, let's get some lemonade before we have to move more stuff," I say. "Come on."

We jump to our feet and hurry over. Reverend Ashford sets the cups down on the table, then rests his hand flat on it and stands still for a minute. He looks very tired. He breathes heavily a few times and goes off to sit in a lawn chair. I'm watching him carefully to see if he needs help.

"These people are old," Brandon whispers nervously.

I nod. "Plus he's sad because he had to move here,"

I say. "He used to have a big church with hundreds of people in it. And he had a big house with maple trees around it for shade. And he liked to feed the birds. He's got a lung disease now, though."

"I've seen you out walking him early in the morning. That's pretty nice of you," Brandon says.

"Yeah. Well, he can't go to the store by himself, so I help him out."

We pour lemonade for us kids and go back to the grass. I figure I have to ask about his mom again. "Is your mom better?"

"Yeah! The doctors said she can probably come home next weekend."

"That's great." I hold up my hand for a high five. He misses, but not by much.

"You know Greg?" Brandon whispers.

I hate whispering. Why won't he talk? Still, I have to snort. Do I know Greg?

"How could I not know Greg? He beat me up, Brandon, remember?"

"Okay. Do you think Greg is in a gang?"

"No way," I burst out. Then I stop to think. Maybe that's why he had three other kids with him. Maybe that's why all the boys do whatever he says. Maybe that's why I should think twice about standing up to him. Well, guess what? It's too late. What's done is done.

"I don't know. It's possible, I guess."

"Well, why is he so mean?" Brandon asks. Then he says, "I told my dad what happened."

"Oh, yeah? Is your dad mad at me for stepping on part of your robot?"

"No. Of course not. He wants me to help you out with something. In return."

"Well, you could teach me chess—I guess I'd like that." I flop straight back in the grass and stare up at the sky.

"Actually, I know your mom made you sign up for soccer. And I know you fought those guys for me. So I'm—I had my dad call—I'm going to soccer, too. Just to watch at first. Just so you'll have a friend there. And maybe, if I practice, I could play a little."

Brandon stares at the grass the whole time. He never looks up at me.

"You?" I ask him. "You're going to soccer?"

But you're such a skinny-bean, I want to yell. You'll pass out. You'll faint. You can't run up and down the field. No way!

"Yeah. My dad already talked to Mr. Olson."

"Well, gosh. Thanks!"

"And you know what? When he talked to Mr. Olson?"

"What? Don't tell me. They had the baby."

"No. But they almost did."

"That's impossible. At least I think that's impossible. How can you almost have a baby? Either you do, or you don't."

"I don't know."

Brandon and I look at each other. The mysteries of grownups' bodies are so weird. Marriage is odd. Sex is impossible to think of. And babies are beyond odd. And then there's the terrible thought that every single person on earth was a baby at one time. Even people in jail were babies. Think of all the diapers.

"Boys, these hot dogs are ready," calls Miss Williams, waving a long-handled fork like a conductor.

"Look at her, you guys. She's doing the Barbecue Symphony. Okay!" I holler.

I turn to Brandon. "She does tai chi."

"Yeah?"

"She's teaching me."

"I'll have a hot dog," Reverend Ashford says, getting up from his lawn chair and practically pushing people aside so he can go stand next to Miss Williams. He loads her plate up with chips and some spicy salsa and escorts Miss Williams to a chair. Man, he really likes her.

"Don't you give *me* any of that peppery salsa, Reverend, or I'll be up all night. Salsa gives me gas. My stomach can't take it," Mrs. Johnson calls out. She piles her plate with the quivery red Jell-O. "Now, this stuff goes down easy. Just what the doctor ordered."

For some reason, this strikes me as funny. We kids start to giggle hysterically, the kind of giggling that, once it starts, just won't stop.

"This salsa gives me gas," Brandon squeals.

Uncle Tim comes over with the lemonade pitcher. "What's this giggling over here?" he asks. "Anyone want a refill?"

We all hold our cups up. I can drink about three gallons of lemonade in one sitting.

Then Walter Ashford comes out the back door, carrying a platter of uncooked ribs and a squeeze bottle full of barbecue sauce. My mother's face lights up and she goes over to say hi.

He puts down the platter, slides his arm around her waist, and pulls her to him, giving her a hug and a kiss on the cheek. I can't stand this! I hate kissy scenes—especially when it's my mother who's involved.

Brandon nudges me. "Who's that?"

"He's the Reverend's son."

"He and your mother are in love!"

I glare at him.

"Hey, Mama!" I yell. "When do we eat?"

She sighs at the interruption. But then she laughs. "We're eating, Junebug."

After the barbecue, the grownups sit talking until all the coals have died down and the sun has set, a red ball sliding down the sky and into the earth like a coin going into a bank. Gotta save some sun for tomorrow.

Later I stop by Miss Williams's apartment, and she invites me in.

"Why don't you sit on my futon? This is my corner for relaxation."

She's got ferns and a fish tank, and a big wicker futon chair. It *is* a relaxing place to sit. A fan is blowing a cool breeze on my hot, tired feet. My toes like it.

"Tasha told me that you kids had been in a nasty fight at school."

"She told you?" I ask indignantly.

"Well, look at it from her point of view. Here she is, six years old, and her wonderful older brother is attacked by four kids, kicking and beating him. Then her brother tells her she can't talk about it. Think how frightened she must have been."

"Yeah. I guess that's true. I was being pretty selfish. And now Mama's signed me up for soccer. All those kids are on the team. Tomorrow, at nine o'clock, we'll all be up at the soccer field. Oh, man."

"So," she says. "A difficult situation. But you will have to face it. Think of your goal and your method to reach that goal. Ancient Tao philosophy contains both together, the complete balance of yin and yang. Your goal is to defeat or disarm this bigger boy, Greg, to turn his own power against him."

"Yeah!"

"Your method must be soft force, giving. Allowing him the chance to defeat himself. If you must, defeat him by force. But perhaps an opportunity will arise where you can allow him to defeat himself."

"Cool. How did you learn this?"

"I decided that I wanted to travel. And I am a very small person. It would be easy for someone to attack me. So I learned some self-defense, but then I became more interested in the Tao approach. Now stand up. We'll practice a few blocks. And I'll teach you one self-defense move, but you'll have to practice it. The thing about it is distance, how far you are from your opponent. Before he expects it, you step in closer. Then you're in control."

Later that night, I lie in bed, thinking about soccer. I visualize my self-defense move. Relax. Block his punch. Step in. Knock him with my hip. Grab his shoulders. Trip. I'll practice every spare moment tomorrow. So if Greg starts another fight, I'll be at least a little prepared. Miss Williams says when most people fight, they flail away madly. That's why, if you step in close, you can easily throw them off-balance.

I always thought that once I started sailing, my life would get easy. There'd be nothing in it except me and a boat. It didn't work that way. Instead, with moving here, starting the new school, worrying about Walter and Mama and my dad, and about Greg, everything seems to me more and more complicated.

But, hey! Brandon comes through! Go, Brandon! What a guy. He's coming to soccer to back me up. Imagine that puny kid thinking he's ready to fight kids like Greg and Darryl. I have to smile at that.

Sixteen

Monday. This is it.

Reverend Ashford is waiting for me. Instead of going for a walk, we go to the little bench. I take the horse stance, bending slowly at the knees to stretch and relax. I breathe slowly and deeply.

"I'd like to get my hands on this fella Greg myself," Reverend Ashford mutters. "I'd like to meet his parents."

"Not me," I say. "I don't want to meet any part of him I don't have to."

I place one leg forward, all my weight on my back foot, and put my arms up in a block position. Then I step quickly forward and shift my weight to the side. There! I'd be in close. That's how I would knock him off-balance. Then I'd just have to trip him.

"That looks good," says Reverend Ashford. "Pretty snazzy."

"Yeah? Want to be Greg? You could stand in front of me."

Reverend Ashford stands still, facing me, arms at his sides. "Now, don't rush at me," he says. "Take it easy."

"Okay."

I close my eyes and visualize what I'm going to do. Then I start. Block. Step in. Hip knock. Shoulder grab. And trip. But I fake the moves.

Miss Williams comes trotting up the street and watches us. "You're doing great, Reeve. Stay relaxed and focused. Make him wear himself out. Don't use more force than necessary."

She gives me a big smile. Then I look down the street. Oh, man. Here comes Brandon. I can't believe he thinks he can help me. How? Still, I have to admire him for coming. He must be scared out of his mind!

At nine, we go up to the school playing field, me dragging my hot feet in my big, clunky basketball sneakers every step of the way. It's a kind of cloudy day, not thunderstorm clouds, but high, even ones. Boring, flat ones. Brandon is trailing along behind me like a dried-up snail.

And there they are—Darryl, Greg, and a bunch of their globby friends bouncing soccer balls on the tops of their heads to show off. They all wear maroon soccer shorts with white trim, and soccer shoes. I don't. Soccer shoes are low and flat and cost thirty-five dollars. It told where to buy them on the sign-up sheet. But we don't have a car and Mama said we ask Walter and Harriet for too many favors already, so that was that.

I don't see Mr. Olson anywhere. Maybe his wife is still almost having the baby. So I walk right up and introduce myself to Darryl's dad, Mr. Mackenzie.

Behind me, Greg snickers when I say my name. "Well, look who's here. I can't believe it. You brought Brandon," he says.

"Are you playing?" Mr. Mackenzie asks Brandon.

Brandon shakes his head. "Not today."

"Mr. Olson and his wife are at the hospital today, although she hasn't had the baby yet," Darryl's dad says. "So I'll be filling in. Okay, everyone. Around the field, fellas. Once!" he yells.

He has a kind of British accent.

I look for Darryl. "Hey, Darryl, where's your dad from?"

"Jamaica."

Jamaica. I've heard that name. I've seen it on my ocean maps. "Isn't that an island kind of near Florida?"

"Yeah!" Darryl gives me a big smile. "You know where it is! Hey, Dad, Reeve knows where Jamaica is."

"Let me shake your hand, young man," Mr. Mackenzie says. "What's your name again?"

"Junebug," I answer before I realize what I'm saying.

"That's easy to remember," he says.

Meanwhile, the other kids start groaning and falling on the ground, complaining about running. "It's too far. It's too hot. We'll never make it."

Lucky they don't work in the boatyard. Ron would not be pleased. I start running. One minute later, that's when I learn how big the soccer field is. Those wavy white lines marked on the grass go on forever. And now, because I started running, the others have to do it, too, so they won't look bad.

Even with the cloudy sky, the weather is hot and damp. Somehow I make it all the way around. I get back to the coach first. Brandon is sitting on the ground by the water cooler. He looks hot also, and he's just sitting there.

"Are you familiar with the game at all?" Mr. Mackenzie asks me.

"Nope."

"Let's start you as goalie, then. We really need someone to take that position."

He tosses me some shin guards to strap on. Then he sets up a row of orange cones. We have to dribble up and around the cones in a figure eight. Not once but time after time after time.

I sit on the ground, strapping on the shin guards.

Greg comes over. "Who said you were goalie?"

"Hmm. Let me think. Santa Claus." I smile at him. I refuse to get angry.

Looks like things are going to come to a head sooner rather than later. I get to my feet quickly. I would at least like to start the fight standing up.

I get in line, not Greg's, to do the drill, dribble around the cones, and come back. Darryl's dad takes half of the kids onto the field to practice overhead passes.

I'm coming back from the cone, kicking the ball a little way in front of me, trying to remember not to punt it like in football and to use the inside of my feet. I'm concentrating on ball control. If Mr. Mackenzie comes over, I want him to see that I'm going all out for this. Then suddenly my left leg goes out from under me, and I fall face-flat on the ground. Greg tripped me.

Oof! So much for soft force! Greg's laughing, pointing at me.

I whirl around and sit up, keeping my eyes on him. I hear Miss Williams's words. "Stay relaxed and focused. Make him wear himself out. Don't use more force than necessary."

The other kids laugh along with Greg.

Mr. Mackenzie is walking over to his van, unloading a huge jug of water, his back to us. I sit there for a minute, looking up at everybody. I look at Greg as I get to my feet. I slow down my breathing and get control.

I feel relaxed and calm. I stare at him intently as I stand up.

He hates it. "What? What are you looking at? Cut it out."

"No. I won't cut it out. Listen, Greg, stay away from me. Four on one? That's sad. That's pitiful. Is that the best you can do? Four on one?"

Still I don't stop. I keep staring. I feel my feet on the ground, like a tree, collecting energy, and now I'm ready. I sense the other kids getting uneasy. I move closer.

Then, blindly, he throws his first punch, wide-armed, way out in front of his body, just the way Miss Williams said he would. I raise my arm and I block it and quickly move in close.

I step forward with my left foot right next to him. My right hip knocks him sideways off-balance. I bring my right foot up, take hold of his shoulders, and swing my leg across the back of his knees. His legs come up together, and down he goes on his back. He falls hard. I can see the tears in his eyes, and I feel bad for a moment. I never hurt someone on purpose before. But if he trips me, I'll return it. No more, no less.

Then, while he's still lying there on the ground, I tear off the shin guards and walk over to Coach

Mackenzie. I'm not doing this. I'm out of here. That's all there is to it.

"I'm done for today. I guess I'll come back tomorrow," I say over my shoulder.

Maybe I will. Maybe I won't. If Mama wants to punish me for not coming back, then that's okay. I'll take the punishment, even if it lasts eight weeks.

"Hey, wait! What happened? Come on, now," Coach Mackenzie says. "Come back. Tell me what happened. Come on, Junebug. We need you!"

The kids are glancing at one another uneasily. They never thought I'd really leave. I shrug, but I keep right on walking. I figure if they really need me, they'll apologize and stop being Greg's little kiss-ups.

Brandon's tearing after me, yelling, "Wait up! Wait for me! Oh, my God, Junebug, it was awesome how you took him down like that. That was so cool! It was just like a karate movie."

As I head down the hill, I can't help but smile a little.

Thank God for Miss Williams! And now Brandon knows my name. He must have heard it at the barbecue, but I guess he figures if the coach can use it, he can, too.

That night, the phone rings. It's for me. It's Darryl's dad.

"I'm sorry about what happened at practice today.

I understand that there was an incident—and that it wasn't the first. I'd like you to talk with Darryl, okay?"

"Okay. I guess."

Darryl gets on. "Hey, Reeve. I'm really sorry."

But that's not good enough. I'm a stickler. I want to know exactly what he's saying. "Sorry for what?" I ask.

"I'm sorry that we ganged up on you at school and that Greg tripped you today."

"Yeah? When your friend acts like a jerk and fights dirty, you need to tell him where to get off. How come you let that kid run your life?"

"I don't know," he mumbles.

"You're scared of him, aren't you?"

"Well, yeah. Everybody is. Hey, how come my dad calls you Junebug? Was that your nickname at your old school? Junebug, that's cool. So are you coming tomorrow?"

"Yeah, I'll be there."

"And guess what? Mr. Olson's wife had the baby."

"Yeah? Awesome!"

Seems like having that baby took forever. I'll never do something like that when I grow up, that's for sure.

When I hang up, Mama says, "What's up? What happened today at soccer?"

I tell her. Straight out. "This kid has been picking on me. Well, me and Brandon. He tripped me while

I was running. And I told him off, and I used a self-defense move that Miss Williams showed me."

"You did? Is he hurt?"

"No. I wasn't trying to hurt him. I just want him to leave us alone."

Mama stares at me.

I smile at her. "Don't worry. That was the coach. It's all taken care of."

"It is?"

I smile some more. "Yeah. It is."

But on Tuesday morning, things don't seem so bright. There's always the gang business to worry about, for one thing. It could be true. Greg getting revenge. He's a pretty crazy kid.

Out walking Reverend Ashford, I hardly notice the tracks, the street, how hot it is. I'm kicking pebbles all the way down Bellmore to the store.

"That was a nice party your mother put on the other night," the Reverend says.

"Huh?"

"What's with you today, young man?"

"I don't know. I don't want to go to soccer, I guess."

"Ridiculous," he says. "How did it go yesterday?"

"Oh. That kid Greg tripped me when I wasn't looking. So I told him off. And then I used the moves Miss Williams taught me." I grin at Reverend Ashford. "He hit the ground pretty hard."

"Ha!"

"But now I don't know. He's pretty wacked-out. I mean, just cause I knocked him down doesn't mean he's going to change."

Reverend Ashford shakes his head. "Boot camp," he mutters. "Ought to put kids like that in boot camp. A lot of kids nowadays don't give a damn about other people. Not a damn."

I stare at him. The Reverend's swearing! But he's kind of forgotten that I'm there.

We sit on the bench. He does the crossword. I look at the baseball scores, even though I told Walter I don't like baseball.

At nine o'clock, I walk up the hill to soccer and meet Darryl's dad. Mr. Mackenzie. Again he's all by himself. No Mr. Olson. I guess Mr. Olson's wife needs him. All the kids are disappointed.

Today we do exercises and stretches. Tomorrow is more running, and then tryouts for positions. Our first game is Thursday. Mr. Mackenzie keeps Greg with him nearly all the time.

Next morning, when the Reverend and I are out walking, I give a big sigh. I'm worried again. I feel so confused. It isn't just soccer that I have to get used to.

I've been feeling bad since the night of the barbecue. I keep remembering Walter and Mama eating their ice cream and cake. It bothers me because they looked so comfortable together. They looked like married people, for Pete's sake! But I can't talk to Mama about it. And I still haven't said anything about Reverend Ashford's cigarettes. I've been worrying more about that, too, since the barbecue.

I never told Mama about the fight at school, either, and that messed up a big chunk of my summer. I have to go to soccer practice every day now, without ever being able to tell Mama why I don't want to go.

When the Reverend and I sit down on the bench, sucking on some powerfully flavored eucalyptus cough mints that I don't really like, I ask, "Is not telling someone something the same as lying? It's not, is it?"

He puts down the sports section of the morning paper. I'm wearing the classifieds on my head, folded into a Napoleon hat. I made this one myself.

"Good question. I'd have to think about it. The thing with lying, the problem with it, is not the lie so much as the reason you have for doing it. If you lie to a bank robber and that lie ends up saving your life, that would be a good lie, wouldn't it?"

"Yeah."

"But you don't know any bank robbers. So that's out. Now let's take Tasha. Not telling something to Tasha might be a wise idea because she's still too little to understand everything. So I guess there can be good lies."

And then suddenly my problem tumbles out. "Whenever I see Walter hanging around my mom, I think what if my dad, my real dad, walked in right now? What would he do?"

I look at Reverend Ashford to see what he's thinking, but he's staring straight ahead.

"My mom doesn't want us to talk about him anymore. Two years ago, he sent me and Tasha a postcard of the Statue of Liberty. Mama threw it out, but I found it and kept it. Mostly I forget all about him. They got divorced and stuff. But then I see Walter, and Walter's not my dad, and I start wondering all over again. I think things like—is my dad tall? Will I be tall like him? And what does his voice sound like? Stuff like that."

I wonder if I look like my dad. Whenever I try to imagine myself as a grownup, I can't. My imaginary crystal ball goes blank. It's like a great big hole.

I look at Reverend Ashford. Does he understand what I'm saying? He's sitting very still. Does he hear me? Maybe he's angry because I don't like Walter enough, but I can't help it. It's a question of loyalty. First come, first served. That's just how kids do it.

Reverend Ashford lays his hand on my shoulder. "This isn't telling a lie so much as keeping a secret, not being open. Keep trying to talk to your mama. When people keep secrets from each other in a family, it can hurt worse than lying. Usually"—he coughs—"we keep secrets about things we're ashamed of. Listen, you got any soccer games coming up soon?" He gives my shoulder a little shake.

"Yeah. Tomorrow at ten o'clock. We play Farrington, grade five. Our first game."

"How would you like some company?" he asks.

"You think you could go to my soccer game? But it's up the hill past the bakery."

"I know where it is," he says, starting to get testy, which he does any time you try to tell him something he knows about.

"You think Mama will let you walk all the way up there alone?" I ask.

"Course she will."

Now he's not only testy, he's getting stubborn—just like the people in my family, including me.

Seventeen

Thursday morning, the air is steamy and muggy. And Reverend Ashford is walking kind of slow. He doesn't even buy a pack of cigarettes. Instead, he buys gum.

After we get back from our walk, I dawdle around till a quarter of nine. Last night Mama said she and Tasha would come to the game for sure.

But during the night Mrs. Johnson's indigestion was acting up, and Mama had to go down to her apartment a couple of times. And early today Mrs. Johnson's doctor is supposed to come. So I guess it's just Tasha who's coming to the game. I told Mama that I don't care. I told her it doesn't matter. But that's not true.

As soon as Brandon comes, we go bang on the Reverend's door. He opens it a crack.

"Are you ready?" I ask. "Come on!"

"You go on ahead. I'll follow," he says.

"Are you sure . . ."

"Go on!" He shuts the door.

"Okay," I say, shrugging. Then I change my mind. "Hey, Brandon, why don't you wait here and come with him."

Tasha and I set out up the hill. It's another stuffy day without a puff of wind anywhere. I'm doing okay at goalie now. And Greg has stopped insulting me, and Darryl's actually trying to be nice. But I'm glad I had it out with Greg on Monday.

Our first game is against one of the hardest teams. Single elimination against the other middle grades! Mr. Olson's supposed to come today. His wife might bring the baby. Her name is Amanda. The boys on the team are pretty upset. They knew it would be a girl. But still. They feel let down.

Darryl's dad is already unloading their van. The tailgate's open and he's lifting out a big cooler of water, enough for both teams.

"We have to win, Junebug," he says. "This is one of the toughest teams. If we beat them, we'll have a good chance of staying in all the way through to the finals. The pressure's on, kid."

I give him a halfhearted grin.

Basically, what he's saying is that if we lose, it will be my fault! Oh, good. It's no wonder no one wants to be goalie. Anyway, I thought Mr. Olson said soccer was about teamwork. Now all I can think about is screwing up, and it makes me nervous.

The other kids on the team start to gather near the van. Everyone's taking a little cup of water and dumping it on top of his head. It feels good. I look around for Reverend Ashford, but he's still not here. Then I catch a glimpse of Brandon slowly coming up the hill. Reverend Ashford is right behind him. I wave. Brandon waves back.

And now here comes Mr. Olson! All right! The kids race over. They mob his car and cling to the door as he tries to climb out.

"Okay, okay. Give me some air, fellas. The baby's fine. No, I didn't bring her this time. So what's up? I heard you guys are awesome."

Everyone's jumping in the air and showing off. I know we're all going to do our best. I can stop goals, nothing to it. I'm ready. I trot off to the net and do my stretching over there. Oh, no. Greg's playing fullback today and yelling and showing off like crazy.

The guys line up. Tasha wanders onto the field with me. "You can't stay here, you know," I tell her.

"I know."

"Go on over and stand with Brandon, okay?"

Mr. Mackenzie's counting heads. And there aren't enough to go around. We're one guy short.

"We could try to play without a goalie and hope they don't notice!" Greg hollers.

Brandon and Reverend Ashford have just reached the field.

Mr. Olson looks around. "Hey, Brandon! How about it? Come on! You can play goalie. We'll put Reeve and Greg at fullback. They'll cover for you. Those two hulks can stop anything. Here, put these guards on." Mr. Olson tosses the shin guards to Brandon and hurries off.

"Get your little ratty sister off the field," Greg says, jogging over to me. "And get your ratty little friend out of goalie. I'll cover it."

"Shut up."

"Junebug, can you help me put this protective stuff on?" Brandon asks.

Brandon's sitting on the ground, struggling with all the unfamiliar straps. He's shaking like a leaf. I kneel beside him.

"Sure. Listen, Brandon, relax. The ball should never even get down here. If it does, that means the rest of your team screwed up, not you. It'll be okay. Lots better than having to run up and down the field on a day like this."

Then I hear Tasha yelling. "Junebug!"

Where is she? I whirl around, looking for her. There she is, with Reverend Ashford, over behind our goal.

"Junebug!"

Why is she calling me? I don't have time to find out.

"Go, Brandon!" yells Reverend Ashford. "We're right behind ya!"

With a loud squeal of the ref's whistle, the game starts. In seconds, Farrington has the ball down at our end of the field. Wow! They are good. Their left wing shoots about ten seconds into the game. I knock it down without a problem.

"Good one, McClain!" yells Darryl's dad.

"Go, Junebug!" yells Brandon. I know he's relieved it didn't come anywhere near him.

I glance over. I can see Reverend Ashford punching the air with his fist behind the goalie's net. I don't have time to smile right now, but I'll store one up for later when I think back on the game.

Finally, our offense gets the ball, and all the action shifts to the far end of the field. This is my biggest problem. When nothing's going on, I start to daydream. It's a bad habit. I do a cartwheel to wake myself up.

"Hey, what are you doing?" yells Darryl's dad. "Come on, Junebug! Be ready down there. Be ready."

Suddenly there is a weak burst of cheering from our fans. Darryl scored. Darryl's a good player. But Greg isn't. He can't run anywhere near fast enough. He's built like a truck.

Okay. Back to the center line. Pay attention,

Junebug. Don't space out. Fierce action midfield. Stay with it.

Greg hangs back. "Help 'em out, Greg!" I yell. "Move up. Boot it. Keep it away from Brandon."

Greg glares at me. "Shut up."

I move forward away from the cage. I try to stay light on my feet so I can jump to either side at the last minute. My knees are bent, my arms loose. I am a bending tree. At that moment, their forward wing blows right through Greg. Right through him! But that's okay. I'm in position. I'm ready for the block. Then their guy passes across in front of me, and their opposite wing boots it behind me. He boots it in and scores. I was nowhere near the ball. Neither, of course, was Brandon.

"Way to blow it for us, you guys!" Greg hollers.

"Don't worry about it, Brandon!" I yell.

The game stays tied at one to one all the rest of the way through the first half. At break, everyone races to the water jug. It sure is hot today.

After I get a drink, I trot over to where Brandon and Reverend Ashford are standing.

"Hey, I guess I really blew it out there," Brandon says. He's close to tears.

"No way," I say. "You were great. Wait till I tell your mom."

"You didn't blow it. Your fullback did, letting that kid dribble right through him. Pitiful," Reverend Ashford says, but his voice sounds weaker than usual. Then he coughs and has to double over.

"Are you okay?" I ask, glancing at Brandon to see if he's noticed anything.

"I was trying to tell you," Tasha says, glaring at me.

"Get back in the game! Get back in the game!" Reverend Ashford says. "I'm fine."

The Reverend's voice sounds grumpy now. Well, that's good. I guess he's okay. I hurry back to the field.

The game starts up. Now their offense is in high gear, which is bad news for me. We don't have much defense. Everyone sort of hangs back and waits for me to stop it. As if I'm an octopus with a billion arms. Still, I'm pretty fired up. It's great having fans at the game.

They score. It's 2 to 1, going into the final seven minutes.

Now we're down at their goal. Darryl's struggling, looking for an opening. Out of the corner of my eye, I see Greg move back.

"You lost the game for us, you know that?" he hollers in Brandon's face. Then he sucker-punches Brandon right in the stomach when he thinks no one's looking, when he thinks everyone is watching Darryl's fancy footwork down at the opposite goal. Brandon doubles over.

Before I realize what I'm doing, I'm over there.

"What?" Greg yells at me. "Get back in position. I didn't do anything."

breathing, there's nothing else I'm supposed to do. Just talk to him. That's the most important thing. Tell him someone went for help. I did that. Let him know I'm there.

"You're doing good, Reverend. It's just a very hot day to come all this way. And then Greg had to be such a creep. Lucky I had Miss Williams to help me and give me advice, huh? Now, don't worry. We're going to take care of this."

He moves his hand over a tiny bit and pats my hand, which is resting on his. Mama was right. He can hear me. He looks just a little better.

Now Darryl's mother is coming. And I see the ambulance tearing up the hill, red lights flashing, but no siren. It drives right onto the playing field. Behind us, the kids get up and hurry over. They gather around in a circle, watching.

"Is this your grandfather, Junebug?" Darryl's mother asks.

"No. My friend."

I lean over close to his ear and whisper, "Don't worry, Reverend Ashford. Next week, you and I are going to be out going for a walk first thing. You're gonna meet me out front, same as always, all right?"

Reverend Ashford gives my hand a little squeeze, so I know he heard.

I plant my feet and take a deep breath. "Hit me, not him, if you're so cool. Go on. Hit me."

"Okay, you jerk. You asked for it."

By now the game has stopped. Greg glances around, hoping for support from his buddies. None of the kids move. The ref's whistle is screeching for us to stop, but the ref is still far, far away. Then Greg hauls off with all his might and swings his arm, trying to slug me in the upper chest. I block his punch with a quick upward swing of my right arm, stepping toward him at the same time. Greg is wide open now. I punch him in the stomach just the way he hit Brandon. I swing my right leg through, grab his shoulders, and flip him back really hard, harder than last time. Greg falls heavily to the ground. I hear the thud. The wind is knocked out of him and he can't talk.

By now Tasha and Reverend Ashford and Darryl's dad have reached us. Mr. Olson runs after them.

"What on earth's going on?" says Mr. Mackenzie angrily, running up to us. "Greg? Junebug?"

"I saw the whole thing," says Reverend Ashford. He points at Greg. "This player ought to be suspended."

"Greg!" yells Mr. Olson. "Off the field! *Now!*"

I've never seen him so angry.

"But Brandon lost the game for us," complains Greg, catching his breath. "He doesn't know what he's doing."

"That's it. We forfeit," Mr. Olson says to the ref.

"Grade five King forfeits. I want this entire team on the bench right now. Off the field, guys."

The kids all come over, their arms hanging, sweat dripping down their necks. Nobody's ever seen Mr. Olson like this before. He's furious.

"How dare you blame this game on a kid who stepped in for us at the last minute? How dare you?" says Mr. Olson.

We all sit in a row on the narrow board bench along the sideline. I'm at the end, feeling guilty as heck. There's dead silence. No one dares look up. Brandon is squeezed over next to me at the end. Bet he's wishing a big mole would come along and dig him a hole in the ground to hide in.

"This team is about two things—teamwork and sportsmanship. If we're going to win games, that's how we'll win them. Otherwise, we deserve to lose." Mr. Olson is staring at each and every kid on the bench. "Otherwise, we *do* lose. Greg, you can consider yourself benched for the next game, if not the play-offs."

Tasha runs up to me and grabs my arm. "Junebug, come quick. You gotta help Reverend Ashford," she whispers.

I look across the field near the goalie cage. Reverend Ashford is doubled over, his hands on his knees, struggling to breathe. I slip off the bench and run over as fast as I can. I lay my hand on his back. I can hear him wheezing.

"You gotta lie down, Reverend," I tell him. "Come on, now."

Gently Tasha and I help him to the ground. Now Mr. Mackenzie is hurrying over.

Reverend Ashford coughs. Then he coughs again. His face is covered with clammy sweat. He should never have come here. I forget all about Greg.

"We've got a cell phone," Mr. Mackenzie says. He sends Darryl for it.

I dial Mama. She says she's calling 911, and to stay with him until she gets there.

Oh God, I wish I'd paid more attention when Mama taught us some emergency treatment. First, talk to him. Talk to him. His lungs are damaged, Mama said. That's all. He's going to be fine. Have him relax.

"Reverend, are you okay? Now, you don't need to worry. Help is on the way, okay?"

He's not completely passed out. He blinks a little. I look up. Brandon's standing beside me. I hope he doesn't faint on us, too.

"A little bit hot today, I guess," I say to the Reverend. "I talked to my mom. She'll be here in a few moments."

I place my cheek down near Reverend Ashford's mouth. He's breathing, but very slowly. Behind me I hear kids grumbling about the game, but I don't care. They have no clue what's going on.

What else did Mama say? Well, as long as he's

I plant my feet and take a deep breath. "Hit me, not him, if you're so cool. Go on. Hit me."

"Okay, you jerk. You asked for it."

By now the game has stopped. Greg glances around, hoping for support from his buddies. None of the kids move. The ref's whistle is screeching for us to stop, but the ref is still far, far away. Then Greg hauls off with all his might and swings his arm, trying to slug me in the upper chest. I block his punch with a quick upward swing of my right arm, stepping toward him at the same time. Greg is wide open now. I punch him in the stomach just the way he hit Brandon. I swing my right leg through, grab his shoulders, and flip him back really hard, harder than last time. Greg falls heavily to the ground. I hear the thud. The wind is knocked out of him and he can't talk.

By now Tasha and Reverend Ashford and Darryl's dad have reached us. Mr. Olson runs after them.

"What on earth's going on?" says Mr. Mackenzie angrily, running up to us. "Greg? Junebug?"

"I saw the whole thing," says Reverend Ashford. He points at Greg. "This player ought to be suspended."

"Greg!" yells Mr. Olson. "Off the field! *Now!*"

I've never seen him so angry.

"But Brandon lost the game for us," complains Greg, catching his breath. "He doesn't know what he's doing."

"That's it. We forfeit," Mr. Olson says to the ref.

"Grade five King forfeits. I want this entire team on the bench right now. Off the field, guys."

The kids all come over, their arms hanging, sweat dripping down their necks. Nobody's ever seen Mr. Olson like this before. He's furious.

"How dare you blame this game on a kid who stepped in for us at the last minute? How dare you?" says Mr. Olson.

We all sit in a row on the narrow board bench along the sideline. I'm at the end, feeling guilty as heck. There's dead silence. No one dares look up. Brandon is squeezed over next to me at the end. Bet he's wishing a big mole would come along and dig him a hole in the ground to hide in.

"This team is about two things—teamwork and sportsmanship. If we're going to win games, that's how we'll win them. Otherwise, we deserve to lose." Mr. Olson is staring at each and every kid on the bench. "Otherwise, we *do* lose. Greg, you can consider yourself benched for the next game, if not the play-offs."

Tasha runs up to me and grabs my arm. "Junebug, come quick. You gotta help Reverend Ashford," she whispers.

I look across the field near the goalie cage. Reverend Ashford is doubled over, his hands on his knees, struggling to breathe. I slip off the bench and run over as fast as I can. I lay my hand on his back. I can hear him wheezing.

"You gotta lie down, Reverend," I tell him. "Come on, now."

Gently Tasha and I help him to the ground. Now Mr. Mackenzie is hurrying over.

Reverend Ashford coughs. Then he coughs again. His face is covered with clammy sweat. He should never have come here. I forget all about Greg.

"We've got a cell phone," Mr. Mackenzie says. He sends Darryl for it.

I dial Mama. She says she's calling 911, and to stay with him until she gets there.

Oh God, I wish I'd paid more attention when Mama taught us some emergency treatment. First, talk to him. Talk to him. His lungs are damaged, Mama said. That's all. He's going to be fine. Have him relax.

"Reverend, are you okay? Now, you don't need to worry. Help is on the way, okay?"

He's not completely passed out. He blinks a little. I look up. Brandon's standing beside me. I hope he doesn't faint on us, too.

"A little bit hot today, I guess," I say to the Reverend. "I talked to my mom. She'll be here in a few moments."

I place my cheek down near Reverend Ashford's mouth. He's breathing, but very slowly. Behind me I hear kids grumbling about the game, but I don't care. They have no clue what's going on.

What else did Mama say? Well, as long as he's

breathing, there's nothing else I'm supposed to do. Just talk to him. That's the most important thing. Tell him someone went for help. I did that. Let him know I'm there.

"You're doing good, Reverend. It's just a very hot day to come all this way. And then Greg had to be such a creep. Lucky I had Miss Williams to help me and give me advice, huh? Now, don't worry. We're going to take care of this."

He moves his hand over a tiny bit and pats my hand, which is resting on his. Mama was right. He can hear me. He looks just a little better.

Now Darryl's mother is coming. And I see the ambulance tearing up the hill, red lights flashing, but no siren. It drives right onto the playing field. Behind us, the kids get up and hurry over. They gather around in a circle, watching.

"Is this your grandfather, Junebug?" Darryl's mother asks.

"No. My friend."

I lean over close to his ear and whisper, "Don't worry, Reverend Ashford. Next week, you and I are going to be out going for a walk first thing. You're gonna meet me out front, same as always, all right?"

Reverend Ashford gives my hand a little squeeze, so I know he heard.

Eighteen

Back at home, I'm sitting on my bed and Tasha's sitting on hers. We're stranded in our bedroom while the nursing-home supervisor is here. I dump all the coins out of my money jar. Plus there's one ten-dollar bill. I want to plant a tree for Reverend Ashford and put it behind the bench. A shade tree for when he comes back.

If he hadn't had to stand out in the hot sun this morning, maybe he wouldn't have collapsed like that.

Reverend didn't tell me the truth. Turns out, he was the one with all the secrets. He didn't tell Mama where he was going today. He didn't tell anybody. And he didn't ever tell anybody about the cigarettes he smoked in the morning. Maybe that made him extra-sick. Maybe he'll die now.

I feel terrible inside, scared to death. I feel as if I

caused everything. I should have told Mama about the cigarettes. But Reverend Ashford's a grownup, as he said. And I'm a kid. I remember him saying people keep secrets about things they're ashamed of. I guess he was ashamed that he smoked.

The nursing-home supervisor is meeting with Mama, reviewing everything, trying to figure out how his breathing got so much worse this past week. They can measure how much air goes in and out of him in the hospital. So, no matter how many packs of mints Reverend Ashford eats to hide the cigarette smell, in the end he's not fooling the doctors.

"But I just don't see how his lung capacity could have gotten so much worse in such a short time," Mama's saying.

I go to the door of the bedroom and open it. I have to tell. He might die. "Mama?"

"What is it?"

"In the mornings, when we go for our walk, Reverend Ashford smokes. He buys cigarettes down at the store. He told me it was okay."

I stand in the doorway, feeling a flood of sadness. I really let Mama down. I guess I shouldn't have listened to him. Will Mama lose her job because of me?

The supervisor is smiling at me. "This isn't your fault at all, Reeve. Reverend Ashford has quite a history of not always telling the truth. If he's going to continue to live here, we've got to find a way to supervise that."

I go back to my room and shut the door. I have a total of $18.76. Is that enough for a shade tree? A little one?

After the supervisor finally leaves, Mama tries to take a nap. She has a tension headache. But she can't sleep much and comes to the kitchen for a glass of iced tea. She hands me a Popsicle. Raspberry.

"So Reverend Ashford came to watch your game?" she says.

I nod. Mama stretches out on the sofa with the fan pointing straight at her head.

"I'm sorry I couldn't go. Here. Sit here," she says, motioning toward the floor.

I sit on the floor and lean back against the edge of the sofa. Mama strokes my forehead. Her palm feels so smooth and soft.

"That's okay," I tell her. I've kind of forgotten how angry I was this morning.

"No, it's not. I'm sorry I've been so busy the past few weeks, Junior. I really am. I know it's been hard on you."

"How's Mrs. Johnson?" I ask.

"Not great. She's having some tests to see if she has an ulcer."

Then Mama says, "I heard the real reason you

didn't want to go to soccer, about those two boys, Darryl and Greg, and how you tried to defend Brandon. How come you didn't tell me about that yourself? It hurt to hear it from someone else."

I shrug. "I don't know. Cause you were so busy, I guess. And you hate fighting so much. Because you think I'll turn into my dad if I get in a fight."

"Can you tell me about it now?"

"I thought you heard it already."

"Not from you. I want to hear you tell it. Not Tasha."

So I tell her about the awful day with the thumbtacks. And the fight. And then I'm thinking about telling her about running on the boatyard dock, even though I know I will never, ever do that again and I came out of it perfectly safely. But no matter what she says, she *is* tired and busy right now. I think it was enough to tell Walter and Reverend Ashford.

The doorbell rings.

"Can you get that, Junior?" she asks.

I hurry to open the door. It's Walter back from the hospital. He reaches down and rubs my head. "Hey, thanks for helping my dad this morning. You were great. He thinks the world of you."

"How's he doing?" I ask.

"Oh, he's on oxygen, which he hates. Says it smells bad and makes his brain feel funny. They're running a lot of tests right now to see what's up with his heart."

Then he straightens up and goes over and hugs

Mama. It's not the kind of hug teachers or even parents give. This is a hug that shows Mama and Walter belong together. Anybody can see that. Even me.

Mama glances my way. She sees me watching.

"Junior," says Mama, "Walter and I are very serious about each other."

Fear thuds into my heart, and this time I can't push it away. We had a dad once. He disappeared a long time ago, and I can hardly remember him at all. But he's still my dad.

She sees how upset I am. "Listen, Junior. When I was eighteen years old, I made a mistake and married your father. But now I don't want you kids to have that kind of father. He's not interested in you. He's not willing to take care of you. It's best for us to move on. We can't change him, Junior. I know that because, believe me, I tried."

She moves to the rocker and puts her face in her hands and massages her forehead. Then the phone rings again and Walter answers it. I listen long enough to hear that Reverend Ashford is improving on the oxygen.

I turn around and go lie flat on my bed. Mama and Walter are still talking to the hospital when I get back up. Tasha is sitting in front of the TV. "I'm going out for a walk," I say.

But no one's listening. Then I head out the front door. I shut it with a quiet click behind me. I'm on my own.

Nineteen

There's only one place for me to go and that's the boatyard. That's where my dreams come true. Well, that's where they used to come true.

Why did I ever think my father was waiting someplace for me, that there was some detail missing—like he didn't know our address?

He's a prisoner, I tell myself. You got that? He's in prison. For ten years. My whole life! My whole life! I scream silently inside my head. And tears run down my face. Prisons have telephones. Prisons have pencil and paper. And I think, but I'm not sure, that prisons have visiting days.

He might be innocent of robbery, but what about never calling me and Tasha? Is he innocent of that? And what if Walter becomes our father? How will he hurt us?

I hurry along Bellmore Avenue, practically running. I think of the parent-child dinner at school, and dads who come yelling their brains out at the soccer field, rooting for their kid above all others. I remember how confident I felt with Brandon and Reverend Ashford cheering me on. I think about how hard Mama has to work.

I stumble along, not paying a whole lot of attention to where I'm going. I know at some point I have to cross under Interstate 95 and go by all the scrap-metal places and train tracks and oil-storage tanks. I start to jog. It's about three miles total to the boatyard.

When I finally get there, it's drizzling lightly and the place is practically empty. It must be well after five o'clock. Here and there inside a few boats, I see the glow of lights, but it's very quiet and spooky. Ron's car is still here, though, parked by the office all by itself.

But, for some reason, I don't go straight inside. Instead, I go to the window and peek in. Ron's sitting at his desk, staring down at the calendar blotter he has. In his hand, he's holding a beer. Another bottle is sitting on the desk.

I draw back from the window. I guess I shouldn't bother him right now. He warned me. He told me this would happen if I hung around a lot. He told me I'd probably see this. Why did it have to be today, when I really need help? Why did he let me down?

And then I think again.

I can't draw Ron into my life. Not every day. No matter how hard I pull and tug, no matter how many sailing trips we take, Ron has his life to live and I have mine, I guess. It's like watching other boats sail past you on the water. Those people are near you, they're doing the same thing, but their lives are different.

I feel a little ashamed of myself for spying on Ron when he thought he was all alone. So I head down the driveway toward the docks. The drizzle is like a fine spray on my face and arms. I pass the place where I fell in the other day. I look at the narrow space between the boat and the dock. That older kid was right. I was lucky not to hit my head. I could have drowned.

Out at the end of the dock is the little sailboat, the *Seagull.* Captain McClain climbs aboard. I try to make myself comfortable among the life jackets. The damp air smells very salty and heavy.

Since we moved, Mama's been trying to tell me what to do, who to be friends with, how to be happy. I guess it's because she's so happy now. She wants the same for me.

I've never really seen Mama happy. I didn't even know it was possible. She's got so much energy that she's like a big water fountain, spraying energy all around. And Walter, he really likes her. I can see that.

But I feel as if I have to protect her and Tasha from

Walter. I don't trust him to take care of us. Why should I? What if he leaves us, too? What if he leaves and never, ever calls? That should be a crime. That's robbery. It's stealing from your own kids, is what it is.

That's one reason, probably, that I liked to pretend Ron was my father. Because he's been working here, in the same place, for twenty years. So he isn't going anywhere. And then because he's already married, he has a grownup kid, and he has the tattooed blue rose to remind him not to drink. He could never really become part of our life. So that made it safe to daydream about.

Walter, on the other hand, he scared me from day one. I knew he was for real. I knew he loved my mama and wasn't going to let her go. I rest my head against the side of the little boat and cry.

Finally, I climb out of the boat and head for the boatyard office. The dark clouds are still blowing past, but it's stopped drizzling. I hurry through the few boats left up on their sawhorses.

There's the big blue boat we scraped a while back. I stop and pat the hull. It's smooth now. All the barnacles scraped off. I run my hand along it, then lay my cheek on it. Secrets are like barnacles, underwater lumps that grow on top of each other, ugly little volcanoes, hard and sharp. Reverend's right, they can hurt your family.

The lights are off in the office now, and Ron's car is gone. Mama must be worried to death. I know where Ron keeps an extra office key, under a brick by the soda machine. Yep. There it is.

I unlock the door and turn on the light, blinking at its brightness. I sit at his desk for a while, until I feel calm enough to call.

I pick up the phone and dial our number. "Mama? It's me. I'm down at the boatyard. I'm sorry."

Mama is so relieved to hear from me. I feel bad that I scared her. But I guess I wanted her to feel scared. Because that's exactly how I felt, thinking about Walter being part of our family.

Walter's going to come get me. Again. He must think I'm a royal pain. I don't really mean to be. But I guess I am. Funny thing is, he doesn't seem to mind. Doesn't seem to mind when he takes care of his dad, either, and Reverend Ashford can be a worse pain in the neck!

I sit at Ron's desk, waiting. In the trash can next to the desk are the two beer bottles, side by side.

I see the pickup truck's headlights in the driveway. I hop up from the chair and run for the door. I open it and let Walter in.

"Hi! Thanks for coming to get me. I'm sorry I made you drive around so much," I say, awkward as anything. "I've been feeling kind of bad. I don't know."

"It's going to be okay now. We'll get this all figured

out, I promise. Don't worry," he says. "Your mama and I are real strong. We can pull this off."

He takes my shoulders and looks into my eyes. "You think you can trust me just a little?"

I nod.

He holds me and rubs my back. Then we go out to the truck.

"Look!" Walter says. "The moon's coming up."

After all the rain this afternoon, the breeze feels cool and fresh. The storm clouds are breaking into patches and moving away. I remember that cloudy, windy Saturday when I stepped into a small tippy sailboat out here. I was so scared!

Pale blue clouds lie in a line along the horizon like stretched-out spouting whales. Then the top edge of the moon comes. It's big. Much bigger than usual. First it's a soft orange, but then, as it rises through the whale-clouds, it turns silver and pale, and it grows smaller and smaller, until it's back to its regular size. I don't know if I've ever seen moonrise from start to finish before.

We get into the truck.

"You know what I like?" Walter says. "I like shapes. That's probably why I like sailing. It's all about triangles."

I stare at him in surprise. "You know how to sail?" I ask.

"Yeah," he says, laughing. "I do."

"You mean you might be able to go with me sometime? Because Ron's been kind of busy."

"Sure."

"Maybe you're too busy, though."

"Nope. I'm not too busy."

"Well, how come you never said so? You never said you knew how to sail."

"I thought I'd wait and see when a good time might be."

Oh, man. Grownups.

At home, Mama gives me a huge hug and pulls me over to the sofa. We sit quietly for a minute. I can't think of what to say.

"I'm sorry, Mama."

"I am, too. I want you and Tasha to be safe."

"I was worried Walter might hurt us like Dad did."

"He won't," she says.

"You think we're going to be lucky this time?" I ask.

"Yep. I think so."

Suddenly I smell fresh-baked pizza. The oven timer rings. Walter pats me on the head. He's wearing the potholder glove and Mama's apron tied around his waist.

"You're just in time," he says, "for Walter's homemade pizza. Your server for the evening will be Tasha."

We all go sit at the table. He hands me a big hot piece, gooey with cheese. Walter's a good cook. He and Tasha have set the table with candles and pink napkins. Theo is sitting in one of the chairs, stacked up high on the phone book and some pillows.

"Does Theo have to eat with us?" I ask.

"Yes!" says Tasha, tying a napkin around his neck.

"I hate watching bears eat pizza," I say, teasing.

"Junebug, don't tease him! Theo likes you. Now, be nice."

Walter serves everyone pizza. Mama whizzes around with the salad and the low-fat dressing. I like hi-fat dressing much better.

"Anybody got croutons?" I ask.

"No," says Mama. "Sit and be thankful."

"Now, listen, you two," Walter tells us. "Your mother and I are going to slow this relationship down a little. We've been rushing you guys way too much the past two weeks and that's really not fair."

"But I bet you're going to get married," Tasha says, her eyes big and round.

"Oh, man. Tasha, can't you—" I start to say.

"Well, we might," Mama says quickly. "Someday."

"How about you and I go to a baseball game tomorrow night? The Ravens. Just the two of us," Walter says to me.

Baseball? I don't know. I told him before that the idea doesn't grab me. I've never been into baseball. The players stand around too much.

"I don't think so," I say. "But there is something else I really want to do."

"Oh yeah? What's that?" Walter asks.

"I want to buy a tree for your dad."

"A tree?"

"A tai-chi tree," Tasha says. "Hey! I'm a poet."

"Hush up, Tash. Yeah, I want to get a regular tree. And I want to plant it out front. I need a shovel, too. And a watering can."

Mama looks at Walter. "Uh-oh. I can tell by his voice. Might as well do it, Walter, and do it fast, I'm telling you right now. Because if you don't, he'll bug us nonstop day and night until you do."

"That's right. I will." I smile at Walter. "Which is how I account for my nickname, Junebug. I'm going to buy a maple, I think. A nice, shady maple to plant by the park bench. That should do the trick."